THE LION AND THE UNICORN

Instead . . . buried her face in its folds.

The Lion and the Unicorn

BY

RICHARD HARDING DAVIS

Illustrated by

H. C. CHRISTY

NEW YORK

CHARLES SCRIBNER'S SONS

1899

University Press

John Wilson and Son, Cambridge, U.S.A.

IN MEMORY

OF

MANY HOT DAYS AND SOME HOT CORNERS
THIS BOOK IS

DEDICATED

TO

LT.-COL. ARTHUR H. LEE, R.A.

*British Military Attaché with the United
States Army*

Contents

List of Illustrations

The Lion and the Unicorn

PRENTISS had a long lease on the house, and because it stood in Jermyn Street the upper floors were, as a matter of course, turned into lodgings for single gentlemen; and because Prentiss was a Florist to the Queen, he placed a lion and unicorn over his flower-shop, just in front of the middle window on the first floor. By stretching a little, each of them could see into the window just beyond him, and could hear all that was said inside; and such things as they saw and heard during the reign of Captain Carrington, who moved in at the same time they did! By day the table in the centre of the room was covered with maps, and the Captain sat with a box of pins, with different-colored flags wrapped around them, and amused himself by sticking them in the maps and measuring the spaces in between, swearing meanwhile to himself. It was a selfish amusement, but it appeared to be the Captain's only intellectual pursuit, for at night, the maps were rolled up, and a green cloth was spread across the table, and there was much company and popping of soda-bottles, and little heaps of gold and silver were moved this way and that across the cloth. The smoke drifted out of the open windows, and the laughter of the Captain's guests rang out loudly in the empty street, so that the policeman halted and raised his eyes reprovingly to the lighted windows, and cabmen drew up beneath them and lay in wait, dozing on their folded arms, for the Captain's guests to depart. The Lion and the Unicorn were rather ashamed of the scandal of it, and they were glad when, one day, the Captain went away with his tin boxes and gun-cases piled high on a four-wheeler.

Prentiss stood on the sidewalk and said: " I wish you good luck, sir." And the Captain said: "I'm coming back a Major, Prentiss." But he never came back. And one day — the Lion remembered the day

The Lion and the Unicorn

very well, for on that same day the newsboys
ran up and down Jermyn Street shouting out
the news of "a 'orrible disaster" to the British arms.   It was then that a young lady came
to the door in a hansom, and Prentiss went
out to meet her and led her upstairs.   They
heard him unlock the Captain's door and say,
"This is his room, miss," and after he had
gone they watched her standing quite still by
the centre table.   She stood there for a very
long time looking slowly about her, and then
she took a photograph of the Captain from
the frame on the mantel and slipped it into
her pocket, and when she went out again her
veil was down, and she was crying.   She
must have given Prentiss as much as a sovereign, for he called her "Your ladyship,"
which he never did under a sovereign.

And she drove off, and they never saw her
again either, nor could they hear the address
she gave the cabman.   But it was somewhere
up St. John's Wood way.

After that the rooms were empty for some
months, and the Lion and the Unicorn were
forced to amuse themselves with the beautiful
ladies and smart-looking men who came to

Prentiss to buy flowers and "buttonholes," and the little round baskets of strawberries, and even the peaches at three shillings each, which looked so tempting as they lay in the window, wrapped up in cotton-wool, like jewels of great price.

Then Philip Carroll, the American gentleman, came, and they heard Prentiss telling him that those rooms had always let for five guineas a week, which they knew was not true; but they also knew that in the economy of nations there must always be a higher price for the rich American, or else why was he given that strange accent, except to betray him into the hands of the London shopkeeper, and the London cabby?

The American walked to the window toward the west, which was the window nearest the Lion, and looked out into the graveyard of St. James's Church, that stretched between their street and Piccadilly.

"You're lucky in having a bit of green to look out on," he said to Prentiss. "I'll take these rooms — at five guineas. That's more than they're worth, you know, but as I know it, too, your conscience needn't trouble you."

4

The Lion and the Unicorn

Then his eyes fell on the Lion, and he nodded to him gravely. " How do you do? " he said. " I 'm coming to live with you for a little time. I have read about you and your friends over there. It is a hazard of new fortunes with me, your Majesty, so be kind to me, and if I win, I will put a new coat of paint on your shield and gild you all over again."

Prentiss smiled obsequiously at the American's pleasantry, but the new lodger only stared at him.

" He seemed a social gentleman," said the Unicorn, that night, when the Lion and he were talking it over. " Now the Captain, the whole time he was here, never gave us so much as a look. This one says he has read of us."

"And why not? " growled the Lion. " I hope Prentiss heard what he said of our needing a new layer of gilt. It 's disgraceful. You can see that Lion over Scarlett's, the butcher, as far as Regent Street, and Scarlett is only one of Salisbury's creations. He received his Letters-Patent only two years back. We date from Palmerston."

The lodger came up the street just at that

moment, and stopped and looked up at the Lion and the Unicorn from the sidewalk, before he opened the door with his night-key. They heard him enter the room and feel on the mantel for his pipe, and a moment later he appeared at the Lion's window and leaned on the sill, looking down into the street below and blowing whiffs of smoke up into the warm night-air.

It was a night in June, and the pavements were dry under foot and the streets were filled with well-dressed people, going home from the play, and with groups of men in black and white, making their way to supper at the clubs. Hansoms of inky-black, with shining lamps inside and out, dashed noiselessly past on mysterious errands, chasing close on each other's heels on a mad race, each to its separate goal. From the cross streets rose the noises of early night, the rumble of the 'buses, the creaking of their brakes, as they unlocked, the cries of the "extras," and the merging of thousands of human voices in a dull murmur. The great world of London was closing its shutters for the night, and putting out the lights; and the new lodger from

6

across the sea listened to it with his heart beating quickly, and laughed to stifle the touch of fear and homesickness that rose in him.

"I have seen a great play to-night," he said to the Lion, "nobly played by great players. What will they care for my poor wares? I see that I have been over-bold. But we cannot go back now — not yet."

He knocked the ashes out of his pipe, and nodded "good-night" to the great world beyond his window. "What fortunes lie with ye, ye lights of London town?" he quoted, smiling. And they heard him close the door of his bedroom, and lock it for the night.

The next morning he bought many geraniums from Prentiss and placed them along the broad cornice that stretched across the front of the house over the shop window. The flowers made a band of scarlet on either side of the Lion as brilliant as a Tommy's jacket.

"I am trying to propitiate the British Lion by placing flowers before his altar," the American said that morning to a visitor.

The Lion and the Unicorn

"The British public you mean," said the visitor; "they are each likely to tear you to pieces."

"Yes, I have heard that the pit on the first night of a bad play is something awful," hazarded the American.

"Wait and see," said the visitor.

"Thank you," said the American, meekly.

Every one who came to the first floor front talked about a play. It seemed to be something of great moment to the American. It was only a bundle of leaves printed in red and black inks and bound in brown paper covers. There were two of them, and the American called them by different names: one was his comedy and one was his tragedy.

"They are both likely to be tragedies," the Lion heard one of the visitors say to another, as they drove away together. "Our young friend takes it too seriously."

The American spent most of his time by his desk at the window writing on little blue pads and tearing up what he wrote, or in reading over one of the plays to himself in a loud voice. In time the number of his visitors increased, and to some of these he would

The Lion and the Unicorn

read his play; and after they had left him he was either depressed and silent or excited and jubilant. The Lion could always tell when he was happy because then he would go to the side table and pour himself out a drink and say, " Here 's to me," but when he was depressed he would stand holding the glass in his hand, and finally pour the liquor back into the bottle again and say, "What 's the use of that ? "

After he had been in London a month he wrote less and was more frequently abroad, sallying forth in beautiful raiment, and coming home by daylight.

And he gave suppers too, but they were less noisy than the Captain's had been, and the women who came to them were much more beautiful, and their voices when they spoke were sweet and low. Sometimes one of the women sang, and the men sat in silence while the people in the street below stopped to listen, and would say, " Why, that is So-and-So singing," and the Lion and the Unicorn wondered how they could know who it was when they could not see her.

The lodger's visitors came to see him at all

hours. They seemed to regard his rooms as a club, where they could always come for a bite to eat or to write notes; and others treated it like a lawyer's office and asked advice on all manner of strange subjects. Sometimes the visitor wanted to know whether the American thought she ought to take £10 a week and go on tour, or stay in town and try to live on £8; or whether she should paint landscapes that would not sell, or race-horses that would; or whether Reggie really loved her and whether she really loved Reggie; or whether the new part in the piece at the Court was better than the old part at Terry's, and was n't she getting too old to play " ingénues " anyway.

The lodger seemed to be a general adviser, and smoked and listened with grave consideration, and the Unicorn thought his judgment was most sympathetic and sensible.

Of all the beautiful ladies who came to call on the lodger the one the Unicorn liked the best was the one who wanted to know whether she loved Reggie and whether Reggie loved her. She discussed this so interestingly while she consumed tea and thin

Consumed tea and thin slices of bread.

slices of bread that the Unicorn almost lost
his balance in leaning forward to listen. Her
name was Marion Cavendish and it was
written over many photographs which stood
in silver frames in the lodger's rooms. She
used to make the tea herself, while the lodger
sat and smoked; and she had a fascinating
way of doubling the thin slices of bread into
long strips and nibbling at them like a mouse
at a piece of cheese. She had wonderful
little teeth and Cupid's-bow lips, and she had
a fashion of lifting her veil only high enough
for one to see the two Cupid-bow lips. When
she did that the American used to laugh, at
nothing apparently, and say, " Oh, I guess
Reggie loves you well enough."

" But do I love Reggie?" she would ask
sadly, with her tea-cup held poised in air.

" I am sure I hope not," the lodger would
reply, and she would put down the veil
quickly, as one would drop a curtain over a
beautiful picture, and rise with great dignity
and say, " if you talk like that I shall not
come again."

She was sure that if she could only get
some work to do her head would be filled

with more important matters than whether Reggie loved her or not.

"But the managers seem inclined to cut their cavendish very fine just at present," she said. "If I don't get a part soon," she announced, "I shall ask Mitchell to put me down on the list for recitations at evening parties."

"That seems a desperate revenge," said the American; "and besides, I don't want you to get a part, because some one might be idiotic enough to take my comedy, and if he should, you must play *Nancy*."

"I would not ask for any salary if I could play *Nancy*," Miss Cavendish answered.

They spoke of a great many things, but their talk always ended by her saying that there must be some one with sufficient sense to see that his play was a great play, and by his saying that none but she must play *Nancy*.

The Lion preferred the tall girl with masses and folds of brown hair, who came from America to paint miniatures of the British aristocracy. Her name was Helen Cabot, and he liked her because she was so brave and fearless, and so determined to be inde-

pendent of every one, even of the lodger —
especially of the lodger, who it appeared had
known her very well at home. The lodger,
they gathered, did not wish her to be independent of him and the two Americans had
many arguments and disputes about it, but
she always said, " It does no good, Philip ;
it only hurts us both when you talk so. I
care for nothing, and for no one but my art,
and, poor as it is, it means everything to me,
and you do not, and, of course, the man I am
to marry, must." Then Carroll would talk,
walking up and down, and looking very fierce
and determined, and telling her how he loved
her in such a way that it made her look even
more proud and beautiful. And she would
say more gently, " It is very fine to think that
any one can care for like that, and very
helpful. But unless I cared in the same way
it would be wicked of me to marry you, and
besides — " She would add very quickly
to prevent his speaking again — " I don't
want to marry you or anybody, and I never
shall. I want to be free and to succeed in
my work, just as you want to succeed in your
work. So please never speak of this again."

13

The Lion and the Unicorn

When she went away the lodger used to sit smoking in the big arm-chair and beat the arms with his hands, and he would pace up and down the room while his work would lie untouched and his engagements pass forgotten.

Summer came and London was deserted, dull, and dusty, but the lodger stayed on in Jermyn Street. Helen Cabot had departed on a round of visits to country houses in Scotland, where, as she wrote him, she was painting miniatures of her hosts and studying the game of golf. Miss Cavendish divided her days between the river and one of the West End theatres. She was playing a small part in a farce-comedy.

One day she came up from Cookham earlier than usual, looking very beautiful in a white boating frock and a straw hat with a Leander ribbon. Her hands and arms were hard with dragging a punting pole and she was sunburnt and happy, and hungry for tea.

"Why don't you come down to Cookham and get out of this heat?" Miss Cavendish asked. "You need it; you look ill."

"I'd like to, but I can't," said Carroll. "The fact is, I paid in advance for these rooms, and if I lived anywhere else I'd be losing five guineas a week on them."

Miss Cavendish regarded him severely. She had never quite mastered his American humor.

"But — five guineas — why that's nothing to you," she said. Something in the lodger's face made her pause. "You don't mean——"

"Yes, I do," said the lodger, smiling. "You see, I started in to lay siege to London without sufficient ammunition. London is a large town, and it did n't fall as quickly as I thought it would. So I am economizing. Mr. Lockhart's Coffee Rooms and I are no longer strangers."

Miss Cavendish put down her cup of tea untasted and leaned toward him.

"Are you in earnest?" she asked. "For how long?"

"Oh, for the last month," replied the lodger; "they are not at all bad — clean and wholesome and all that."

"But the suppers you gave us, and this," she cried, suddenly, waving her hands over

The Lion and the Unicorn

the pretty tea-things, "and the cake and muffins?"

"My friends, at least," said Carroll, "need not go to Lockhart's."

"And the Savoy?" asked Miss Cavendish, mournfully shaking her head.

"A dream of the past," said Carroll, waving his pipe through the smoke. "Gatti's? Yes, on special occasions; but for necessity, the Chancellor's, where one gets a piece of the prime roast beef of Old England, from Chicago, and potatoes for ninepence — a pot of bitter twopence-halfpenny, and a penny for the waiter. It's most amusing on the whole. I am learning a little about London, and some things about myself. They are both most interesting subjects."

"Well, I don't like it," Miss Cavendish declared helplessly. "When I think of those suppers and the flowers, I feel — I feel like a robber."

"Don't," begged Carroll. "I am really the most happy of men — that is, as the chap says in the play, I would be if I was n't so damned miserable. But I owe no man a penny and I have assets — I have £80 to last

16

me through the winter and two marvellous plays; and I love, next to yourself, the most wonderful woman God ever made. That's enough."

"But I thought you made such a lot of money by writing?" asked Miss Cavendish.

"I do — that is, I could," answered Carroll, "if I wrote the things that sell; but I keep on writing plays that won't."

"And such plays!" exclaimed Marion, warmly; "and to think that they are going begging." She continued indignantly, "I can't imagine what the managers do want."

"I know what they don't want," said the American. Miss Cavendish drummed impatiently on the tea-tray.

"I wish you wouldn't be so abject about it," she said. "If I were a man I'd make them take those plays."

"How?" asked the American; "with a gun?"

"Well, I'd keep at it until they read them," declared Marion. "I'd sit on their front steps all night and I'd follow them in cabs, and I'd lie in wait for them at the stage-door. I'd just make them take them."

The Lion and the Unicorn

Carroll sighed and stared at the ceiling. "I guess I'll give up and go home," he said.

"Oh, yes, do, run away before you are beaten," said Miss Cavendish, scornfully. "Why, you can't go now. Everybody will be back in town soon, and there are a lot of new plays coming on, and some of them are sure to be failures, and that's our chance. You rush in with your piece and somebody may take it sooner than close the theatre."

"I'm thinking of closing the theatre myself," said Carroll. "What's the use of my hanging on here?" he exclaimed. "It distresses Helen to know I am in London, feeling about her as I do — and the Lord only knows how it distresses me. And, maybe, if I went away," he said, consciously, "she might miss me. She might see the difference."

Miss Cavendish held herself erect and pressed her lips together with a severe smile. "If Helen Cabot doesn't see the difference between you and the other men she knows now," she said, "I doubt if she ever will. Besides — " she continued, and then hesitated.

"Well, go on," urged Carroll.

18

The Lion and the Unicorn

"Well, I was only going to say," she explained, "that leaving the girl alone never did the man any good unless he left her alone willingly. If she's sure he still cares, it's just the same to her where he is. He might as well stay on in London as go to South Africa. It won't help him any. The difference comes when she finds he has stopped caring. Why, look at Reggie. He tried that. He went away for ever so long, but he kept writing me from wherever he went, so that he was perfectly miserable — and I went on enjoying myself. Then when he came back, he tried going about with his old friends again. He used to come to the theatre with them — oh, with such nice girls — but he always stood in the back of the box and yawned and scowled — so I knew. And, anyway, he'd always spoil it all by leaving them and waiting at the stage entrance for me. But one day he got tired of the way I treated him and went off on a bicycle tour with Lady Hacksher's girls and some men from his regiment, and he was gone three weeks and never sent me even a line; and I got so scared; I couldn't sleep, and I stood it for three days more, and then I wired him to come back or I'd jump off London Bridge; and he came back that very night from Edinburgh on the express, and I was so glad to see him that I got confused, and in the general excitement I promised to marry him, so that's how it was with us."

"Yes," said the American, without enthusiasm; "but then I still care, and Helen knows I care."

"Does n't she ever fancy that you might care for some one else? You have a lot of friends, you know."

"Yes, but she knows they are just that — friends," said the American.

Miss Cavendish stood up to go, and arranged her veil before the mirror above the fireplace.

"I come here very often to tea," she said.

"It's very kind of you," said Carroll. He was at the open window, looking down into the street for a cab.

"Well, no one knows I am engaged to Reggie," continued Miss Cavendish, "except you and Reggie, and he is n't so sure. *She* does n't know it."

The Lion and the Unicorn

"Well?" said Carroll.

Miss Cavendish smiled a mischievous kindly smile at him from the mirror.

"Well?" she repeated, mockingly. Carroll stared at her and laughed. After a pause he said: "It's like a plot in a comedy. But I'm afraid I'm too serious for play-acting."

"Yes, it is serious," said Miss Cavendish. She seated herself again and regarded the American thoughtfully. "You are too good a man to be treated the way that girl is treating you, and no one knows it better than she does. She'll change in time, but just now she thinks she wants to be independent. She's in love with this picture-painting idea, and with the people she meets. It's all new to her — the fuss they make over her and the titles, and the way she is asked about. We know she can't paint. We know they only give her commissions because she's so young and pretty, and American. She amuses them, that's all. Well, that cannot last; she'll find it out. She's too clever a girl, and she is too fine a girl to be content with that long. Then — then she'll come back to you. She feels now that she has both you and the others,

and she's making you wait: so wait and be
cheerful. She's worth waiting for; she's
young, that's all. She'll see the difference
in time. But, in the meanwhile, it would
hurry matters a bit if she thought she had
to choose between the new friends and
you."

"She could still keep her friends, and
marry me," said Carroll; "I have told her
that a hundred times. She could still paint
miniatures and marry me. But she won't
marry me."

"She won't marry you because she knows
she can whenever she wants to," cried Marion.
"Can't you see that? But if she thought you
were going to marry some one else now?"

"She would be the first to congratulate
me," said Carroll. He rose and walked to
the fireplace, where he leaned with his arm
on the mantel. There was a photograph of
Helen Cabot near his hand, and he turned
this toward him and stood for some time
staring at it. "My dear Marion," he said at
last, "I've known Helen ever since she was
as young as that. Every year I've loved
her more, and found new things in her to

care for; now I love her more than any
other man ever loved any other woman."

Miss Cavendish shook her head sympa-
thetically.

"Yes, I know," she said; "that's the way
Reggie loves me, too."

Carroll went on as though he had not
heard her.

"There's a bench in St. James's Park,"
he said, "where we used to sit when she first
came here, when she didn't know so many
people. We used to go there in the morning and throw penny buns to the ducks.
That's been my amusement this summer
since you've all been away — sitting on that
bench, feeding penny buns to the silly ducks
— especially the black one, the one she
used to like best. And I make pilgrimages
to all the other places we ever visited together, and try to pretend she is with me.
And I support the crossing sweeper at
Lansdowne Passage because she once said
she felt sorry for him. I do all the other
absurd things that a man in love tortures
himself by doing. But to what end? She
knows how I care, and yet she won't see why

23

we can't go on being friends as we once were.
What's the use of it all?"

"She is young, I tell you," repeated Miss
Cavendish, "and she's too sure of you.
You've told her you care; now try making
her think you don't care."

Carroll shook his head impatiently.

"I will not stoop to such tricks and pretence, Marion," he cried impatiently. "All
I have is my love for her; if I have to cheat
and to trap her into caring, the whole thing
would be degraded."

Miss Cavendish shrugged her shoulders
and walked to the door. "Such amateurs!"
she exclaimed, and banged the door after her.

Carroll never quite knew how he had come
to make a confidante of Miss Cavendish.
Helen and he had met her when they first
arrived in London, and as she had acted for
a season in the United States, she adopted
the two Americans — and told Helen where
to go for boots and hats, and advised Carroll
about placing his plays. Helen soon made
other friends, and deserted the artists, with
whom her work had first thrown her. She
seemed to prefer the society of the people

who bought her paintings, and who admired
and made much of the painter. As she was
very beautiful and at an age when she enjoyed everything in life keenly and eagerly,
to give her pleasure was in itself a distinct
pleasure; and the worldly tired people she
met were considering their own entertainment
quite as much as hers when they asked her
to their dinners and dances, or to spend a
week with them in the country. In her way,
she was as independent as was Carroll in his,
and as she was not in love, as he was, her life
was not narrowed down to but one ideal. But
she was not so young as to consider herself
infallible, and she had one excellent friend
on whom she was dependent for advice and
to whose directions she submitted implicitly.
This was Lady Gower, the only person to
whom Helen had spoken of Carroll and of
his great feeling for her. Lady Gower, immediately after her marriage, had been a
conspicuous and brilliant figure in that set in
London which works eighteen hours a day to
keep itself amused, but after the death of her
husband she had disappeared into the country as completely as though she had entered

25

a convent, and after several years had then
re-entered the world as a professional philan-
thropist. Her name was now associated
entirely with Women's Leagues, with commit-
tees that presented petitions to Parliament,
and with public meetings, at which she spoke
with marvellous ease and effect. Her old
friends said she had taken up this new pose
as an outlet for her nervous energies, and as
an effort to forget the man who alone had
made life serious to her. Others knew her as
an earnest woman, acting honestly for what
she thought was right. Her success, all ad-
mitted, was due to her knowledge of the world
and to her sense of humor, which taught her
with whom to use her wealth and position,
and when to demand what she wanted solely
on the ground that the cause was just.

She had taken more than a fancy for Helen,
and the position of the beautiful, motherless
girl had appealed to her as one filled with
dangers. When she grew to know Helen
better, she recognized that these fears were
quite unnecessary, and as she saw more of her
she learned to care for her deeply. Helen
had told her much of Carroll and of his

double purpose in coming to London; of his brilliant work and his lack of success in having it recognized; and of his great and loyal devotion to her, and of his lack of success, not in having that recognized, but in her own inability to return it. Helen was proud that she had been able to make Carroll care for her as he did, and that there was anything about her which could inspire a man whom she admired so much, to believe in her so absolutely and for so long a time. But what convinced her that the outcome for which he hoped was impossible, was the very fact that she could admire him, and see how fine and unselfish his love for her was, and yet remain untouched by it.

She had been telling Lady Gower one day of the care he had taken of her ever since she was fourteen years of age, and had quoted some of the friendly and loverlike acts he had performed in her service, until one day they had both found out that his attitude of the elder brother was no longer possible, and that he loved her in the old and only way. Lady Gower looked at her rather doubtfully and smiled.

The Lion and the Unicorn

"I wish you would bring him to see me, Helen" she said; "I think I should like your friend very much. From what you tell me of him I doubt if you will find many such men waiting for you in this country. Our men marry for reasons of property, or they love blindly, and are exacting and selfish before and after they are married. I know, because so many women came to me when my husband was alive to ask how it was that I continued so happy in my married life."

"But I don't want to marry any one," Helen remonstrated gently. "American girls are not always thinking only of getting married."

"What I meant was this," said Lady Gower, "that, in my experience, I have heard of but few men who care in the way this young man seems to care for you. You say you do not love him; but if he had wanted to gain my interest, he could not have pleaded his cause better than you have done. He seems to see your faults and yet love you still, in spite of them — or on account of them. And I like the things he does for you. I like, for instance, his sending you the book of the moment every week for two years. That shows a most unswerving spirit of devotion. And the story of the broken bridge in the woods is a wonderful story. If I were a young girl, I could love a man for that alone. It was a beautiful thing to do."

Helen sat with her chin on her hands, deeply considering this new point of view.

"I thought it very foolish of him," she confessed questioningly, "to take such a risk for such a little thing."

Lady Gower smiled down at her from the height of her many years.

"Wait," she said dryly, "you are very young now — and very rich; every one is crowding to give you pleasure, to show his admiration. You are a very fortunate girl. But later, these things which some man has done because he loved you, and which you call foolish, will grow large in your life, and shine out strongly, and when you are discouraged and alone, you will take them out, and the memory of them will make you proud and happy. They are the honors which women wear in secret."

The Lion and the Unicorn

Helen came back to town in September, and for the first few days was so occupied in refurnishing her studio and in visiting the shops that she neglected to send Carroll word of her return. When she found that a whole week had passed without her having made any effort to see him, and appreciated how the fact would hurt her friend, she was filled with remorse, and drove at once in great haste to Jermyn Street, to announce her return in person. On the way she decided that she would soften the blow of her week of neglect by asking him to take her out to luncheon. This privilege she had once or twice accorded him, and she felt that the pleasure these excursions gave Carroll were worth the consternation they caused to Lady Gower.

The servant was uncertain whether Mr. Carroll was at home or not, but Helen was too intent upon making restitution to wait for the fact to be determined, and, running up the stairs, knocked sharply at the door of his study.

A voice bade her come in, and she entered, radiant and smiling her welcome. But

The Lion and the Unicorn

Carroll was not there to receive it, and instead, Marion Cavendish looked up at her from his desk where she was busily writing. Helen paused with a surprised laugh, but Marion sprang up and hailed her gladly. They met half way across the room and kissed each other with the most friendly feeling.

Philip was out, Marion said, and she had just stepped in for a moment to write him a note. If Helen would excuse her, she would finish it, as she was late for rehearsal.

But she asked over her shoulder, with great interest, if Helen had passed a pleasant summer. She thought she had never seen her looking so well. Helen thought Miss Cavendish herself was looking very well also, but Marion said no; that she was too sunburnt, she would not be able to wear a dinner-dress for a month. There was a pause while Marion's quill scratched violently across Carroll's note-paper. Helen felt that in some way she was being treated as an intruder; or worse, as a guest. She did not sit down, it seemed impossible to do so, but she moved uncertainly about the room. She noted that there were many changes, it seemed more bare and empty; her picture was still on the writing-desk, but there were at least six new photographs of Marion. Marion herself had brought them to the room that morning, and had carefully arranged them in conspicuous places. But Helen could not know that. She thought there was an unnecessary amount of writing scribbled over the face of each.

Marion addressed her letter and wrote "Immediate" across the envelope, and placed it before the clock on the mantel-shelf. "You will find Philip looking very badly," she said, as she pulled on her gloves. "He has been in town all summer, working very hard — he has had no holiday at all. I don't think he's well. I have been a great deal worried about him," she added. Her face was bent over the buttons of her glove, and when she raised her blue eyes to Helen they were filled with serious concern.

"Really," Helen stammered, "I — I did n't know — in his letters he seemed very cheerful."

Marion shook her head and turned and

stood looking thoughtfully out of the window. "He's in a very hard place," she began abruptly, and then stopped as though she had thought better of what she intended to say. Helen tried to ask her to go on, but could not bring herself to do so. She wanted to get away.

"I tell him he ought to leave London," Marion began again; "he needs a change and a rest."

"I should think he might," Helen agreed, "after three months of this heat. He wrote me he intended going to Herne Bay or over to Ostend."

"Yes, he had meant to go," Marion answered. She spoke with the air of one who possessed the most intimate knowledge of Carroll's movements and plans, and change of plans. "But he couldn't," she added. "He couldn't afford it. Helen," she said, turning to the other girl, dramatically, "do you know — I believe that Philip is very poor."

Miss Cabot exclaimed incredulously, "Poor!" She laughed. "Why, what do you mean?"

3   33

The Lion and the Unicorn

"I mean that he has no money," Marion answered, sharply. "These rooms represent nothing. He only keeps them on because he paid for them in advance. He's been living on three shillings a day. That's poor for him. He takes his meals at cabmen's shelters and at Lockhart's, and he's been doing so for a month."

Helen recalled with a guilty thrill the receipt of certain boxes of La France roses — cut long, in the American fashion — which had arrived within the last month at various country houses. She felt indignant at herself, and miserable. Her indignation was largely due to the recollection that she had given these flowers to her hostess to decorate the dinner-table.

She hated to ask this girl of things which she should have known better than any one else. But she forced herself to do it. She felt she must know certainly and at once.

"How do you know this?" she asked. "Are you sure there is no mistake?"

"He told me himself," said Marion, "when he talked of letting the plays go and return-

ing to America. He said he must go back;
that his money was gone."

"He is gone to America!" Helen said,
blankly.

"No, he wanted to go, but I would n't let
him," Marion went on. "I told him that
some one might take his play any day. And
this third one he has written, the one he
finished this summer in town, is the best of
all, I think. It 's a love-story. It 's quite
beautiful." She turned and arranged her
veil at the glass, and as she did so, her eyes
fell on the photographs of herself scattered
over the mantelpiece, and she smiled slightly.
But Helen did not see her — she was sitting
down now, pulling at the books on the table.
She was confused and disturbed by emotions
which were quite strange to her, and when
Marion bade her good-by she hardly noticed
her departure. What impressed her most of
all in what Marion had told her, was, she was
surprised to find, that Philip was going away.
That she herself had frequently urged him
to do so, for his own peace of mind, seemed
now of no consequence. Now that he seriously contemplated it, she recognized that

35

his absence meant to her a change in everything. She felt for the first time the peculiar place he held in her life. Even if she had seen him but seldom, the fact that he was within call had been more of a comfort and a necessity to her than she understood.

That he was poor, concerned her chiefly because she knew that, although this condition could only be but temporary, it would distress him not to have his friends around him, and to entertain them as he had been used to do. She wondered eagerly if she might offer to help him, but a second thought assured her that, for a man, that sort of help from a woman was impossible.

She resented the fact that Marion was deep in his confidence; that it was Marion who had told her of his changed condition and of his plans. It annoyed her so acutely that she could not remain in the room where she had seen her so complacently in possession. And after leaving a brief note for Philip, she went away. She stopped a hansom at the door, and told the man to drive along the Embankment — she wanted to be quite alone, and she felt she could see no one until she had thought it all out, and had analyzed the new feelings.

So for several hours she drove slowly up and down, sunk far back in the cushions of the cab, and staring with unseeing eyes at the white enamelled tariff and the black dash-board.

She assured herself that she was not jealous of Marion, because, in order to be jealous, she first would have to care for Philip in the very way she could not bring herself to do.

She decided that his interest in Marion hurt her, because it showed that Philip was not capable of remaining true to the one ideal of his life. She was sure that this explained her feelings — she was disappointed that he had not kept up to his own standard; that he was weak enough to turn aside from it for the first pretty pair of eyes. But she was too honest and too just to accept that diagnosis of her feelings as final — she knew there had been many pairs of eyes in America and in London, and that though Philip had seen them, he had not answered them when they spoke. No, she confessed frankly,

she was hurt with herself for neglecting her
old friend so selfishly and for so long a time;
his love gave him claims on her consideration, at least, and she had forgotten that and
him, and had run after strange gods and
allowed others to come in and take her
place, and to give him the sympathy and
help which she should have been the first
to offer, and which would have counted more
when coming from her than from any one
else. She determined to make amends at
once for her thoughtlessness and selfishness,
and her brain was pleasantly occupied with
plans and acts of kindness. It was a new
entertainment, and she found she delighted
in it. She directed the cabman to go to
Solomons's, and from there sent Philip a
bunch of flowers and a line saying that on
the following day she was coming to take
tea with him. She had a guilty feeling that
he might consider her friendly advances more
seriously than she meant them, but it was her
pleasure to be reckless: her feelings were
running riotously, and the sensation was so
new that she refused to be circumspect or to
consider consequences. Who could tell, she

asked herself with a quick, frightened gasp, but that, after all, it might be that she was learning to care? From Solomons's she bade the man drive to the shop in Cranbourne Street where she was accustomed to purchase the materials she used in painting, and Fate, which uses strange agents to work out its ends, so directed it that the cabman stopped a few doors below this shop, and opposite one where jewelry and other personal effects were bought and sold. At any other time, or had she been in any other mood, what followed might not have occurred, but Fate, in the person of the cabman, arranged it so that the hour and the opportunity came together.

There were some old mezzotints in the window of the loan shop, a string of coins and medals, a row of new French posters; and far down to the front a tray filled with gold and silver cigarette-cases and watches and rings. It occurred to Helen, who was still bent on making restitution for her neglect, that a cigarette-case would be more appropriate for a man than flowers, and more lasting. And she scanned the contents of the

window with the eye of one who now saw in
everything only something which might give
Philip pleasure.   The two objects of value in
the tray upon which her eyes first fell were
the gold seal-ring with which Philip had
sealed his letters to her, and, lying next to it,
his gold watch!   There was something almost human in the way the ring and watch
spoke to her from the past — in the way they
appealed to her to rescue them from the surroundings to which they had been abandoned.
She did not know what she meant to do with
them nor how she could return them to Philip;
but there was no question of doubt in her
manner as she swept with a rush into the
shop.   There was no attempt, either, at bar-
gaining in the way in which she pointed out
to the young woman behind the counter
the particular ring and watch she wanted.
They had not been left as collateral, the
young woman said; they had been sold outright.

"Then any one can buy them?" Helen
asked eagerly. "They are for sale to the
public — to any one?"

The young woman made note of the customer's eagerness, but with an unmoved countenance.

" Yes, miss, they are for sale. The ring is four pounds and the watch twenty-five."

" Twenty-nine pounds ! " Helen gasped.

That was more money than she had in the world, but the fact did not distress her, for she had a true artistic disregard for ready money, and the absence of it had never disturbed her. But now it assumed a sudden and alarming value. She had ten pounds in her purse and ten pounds at her studio — these were just enough to pay for a quarter's rent and the rates, and there was a hat and cloak in Bond Street which she certainly must have. Her only assets consisted of the possibility that some one might soon order a miniature, and to her mind that was sufficient. Some one always had ordered a miniature, and there was no reasonable doubt but that some one would do it again. For a moment she questioned if it would not be sufficient if she bought the ring and allowed the watch to remain. But she recognized that the ring meant more to her than the watch, while the latter, as an old heirloom which had been passed down to him from a great-grandfather, meant more to Philip. It was for Philip she was doing this, she reminded herself. She stood holding his possessions, one in each hand, and looking at the young woman blankly. She had no doubt in her mind that at least part of the money he had received for them had paid for the flowers he had sent to her in Scotland. The certainty of this left her no choice. She laid the ring and watch down and pulled the only ring she possessed from her own finger. It was a gift from Lady Gower. She had no doubt that it was of great value.

"Can you lend me some money on that?" she asked. It was the first time she had conducted a business transaction of this nature, and she felt as though she were engaging in a burglary.

"We don't lend money, miss," the girl said, "we buy outright. I can give you twenty-eight shillings for this," she added.

"Twenty-eight shillings," Helen gasped; "why, it is worth — oh, ever so much more than that!"

The Lion and the Unicorn

"That is all it is worth to us," the girl answered. She regarded the ring indifferently and laid it away from her on the counter. The action was final.

Helen's hands rose slowly to her breast, where a pretty watch dangled from a bowknot of crushed diamonds. It was her only possession, and she was very fond of it. It also was the gift of one of the several great ladies who had adopted her since her residence in London. Helen had painted a miniature of this particular great lady which had looked so beautiful that the pleasure which the original of the portrait derived from the thought that she still really looked as she did in the miniature was worth more to her than many diamonds.

But it was different with Helen, and no one could count what it cost her to tear away her one proud possession.

"What will you give me for this?" she asked defiantly.

The girl's eyes showed greater interest. "I can give you twenty pounds for that," she said.

"Take it, please," Helen begged, as though

43

she feared if she kept it a moment longer she might not be able to make the sacrifice.

"That will be enough now," she went on, taking out her ten-pound note. She put Lady Gower's ring back upon her finger and picked up Philip's ring and watch with the pleasure of one who has come into a great fortune. She turned back at the door.

"Oh," she stammered, "in case any one should inquire, you are not to say who bought these."

"No, miss, certainly not," said the woman. Helen gave the direction to the cabman and, closing the doors of the hansom, sat looking down at the watch and the ring, as they lay in her lap. The thought that they had been his most valued possessions, which he had abandoned forever, and that they were now entirely hers, to do with as she liked, filled her with most intense delight and pleasure. She took up the heavy gold ring and placed it on the little finger of her left hand; it was much too large, and she removed it and balanced it for a moment doubtfully in the palm of her right hand. She was smiling, and her face was lit with shy and tender thoughts. She cast a quick glance to the left and right as though fearful that people passing in the street would observe her, and then slipped the ring over the fourth finger of her left hand. She gazed at it with a guilty smile and then, covering it hastily with her other hand, leaned back, clasping it closely, and sat frowning far out before her with puzzled eyes.

To Carroll all roads led past Helen's studio, and during the summer, while she had been absent in Scotland it was one of his sad pleasures to make a pilgrimage to her street and to pause opposite the house and look up at the empty windows of her rooms. It was during this daily exercise that he learned, through the arrival of her luggage, of her return to London, and when day followed day without her having shown any desire to see him or to tell him of her return he denounced himself most bitterly as a fatuous fool.

At the end of the week he sat down and considered his case quite calmly. For three years he had loved this girl, deeply and

45

The Lion and the Unicorn

tenderly. He had been lover, brother, friend, and guardian. During that time, even though she had accepted him in every capacity except as that of the prospective husband, she had never given him any real affection, nor sympathy, nor help; all she had done for him had been done without her knowledge or intent. To know her, to love her, and to scheme to give her pleasure had been its own reward, and the only one. For the last few months he had been living like a crossing-sweeper in order to be able to stay in London until she came back to it, and that he might still send her the gifts he had always laid on her altar. He had not seen her in three months. Three months that had been to him a blank, except for his work — which like all else that he did, was inspired and carried on for her. Now at last she had returned and had shown that, even as a friend, he was of so little account in her thoughts, of so little consequence in her life, that after this long absence she had no desire to learn of his welfare or to see him — she did not even give him the chance to see her. And so, placing these facts before him for the first time since he had loved her, he considered what was due to himself. "Was it good enough?" he asked. "Was it just that he should continue to wear out his soul and body for this girl who did not want what he had to give, who treated him less considerately than a man whom she met for the first time at dinner? He felt he had reached the breaking-point; that the time had come when he must consider what he owed to himself. There could never be any other woman save Helen, but as it was not to be Helen, he could no longer, with self-respect, continue to proffer his love only to see it slighted and neglected. He was humble enough concerning himself, but of his love he was very proud. Other men could give her more in wealth or position, but no one could ever love her as he did. "He that hath more let him give," he had often quoted to her defiantly, as though he were challenging the world, and now he felt he must evolve a make-shift world of his own — a world in which she was not his only spring of acts; he must begin all over again and keep his love secret and sacred until she understood it and wanted it. And if she should never want it he would at least have saved it from many rebuffs and insults.

With this determination strong in him, the note Helen had left for him after her talk with Marion, and the flowers, and the note with them, saying she was coming to take tea on the morrow, failed to move him except to make him more bitter. He saw in them only a tardy recognition of her neglect — an effort to make up to him for thoughtlessness which, from her, hurt him worse than studied slight.

A new régime had begun, and he was determined to establish it firmly and to make it impossible for himself to retreat from it ; and in the note in which he thanked Helen for the flowers and welcomed her to tea, he declared his ultimatum.

"You know how terribly I feel," he wrote ; "I don't have to tell you that, but I cannot always go on dragging out my love and holding it up to excite your pity as beggars show their sores. I cannot always go on praying before your altar, cutting myself with knives and calling upon you to listen to me.

48

The Lion and the Unicorn

You know that there is no one else but you, and that there never can be any one but you, and that nothing is changed except that after this I am not going to urge and torment you. I shall wait as I have always waited — only now I shall wait in silence. You know just how little, in one way, I have to offer you, and you know just how much I have in love to offer you. It is now for you to speak — some day, or never. But you will have to speak first. You will never hear a word of love from me again. Why should you? You know it is always waiting for you. But if you should ever want it, you must come to me, and take off your hat and put it on my table and say, ' Philip, I have come to stay.' Whether you can ever do that or not can make no difference in my love for you. I shall love you always, as no man has ever loved a woman in this world, but it is you who must speak first; for me, the rest is silence."

The following morning as Helen was leaving the house she found this letter lying on the hall-table, and ran back with it to her rooms. A week before she would have let it lie on the table and read it on her return. She was conscious that this was what she would have done, and it pleased her to find that what concerned Philip was now to her the thing of greatest interest. She was pleased with her own eagerness — her own happiness was a welcome sign, and she was proud and glad that she was learning to care.

She read the letter with an anxious pride and pleasure in each word that was entirely new. Philip's recriminations did not hurt her, they were the sign that he cared; nor did his determination not to speak of his love to her hurt her, for she believed him when he said that he would always care. She read the letter twice, and then sat for some time considering the kind of letter Philip would have written had he known her secret — had he known that the ring he had abandoned was now upon her finger.

She rose and, crossing to a desk, placed the letter in a drawer, and then took it out again and re-read the last page. When she had finished it she was smiling. For a moment she stood irresolute, and then, moving slowly toward the centre-table, cast a guilty look about her and, raising her hands, lifted her veil and half withdrew the pins that fastened her hat.

"Philip," she began in a frightened whisper, "I have — I have come to — "

The sentence ended in a cry of protest, and she rushed across the room as though she were running from herself. She was blushing violently.

"Never!" she cried, as she pulled open the door; "I could never do it — never!"

The following afternoon, when Helen was to come to tea, Carroll decided that he would receive her with all the old friendliness, but that he must be careful to subdue all emotion.

He was really deeply hurt at her treatment, and had it not been that she came on her own invitation he would not of his own accord have sought to see her. In consequence, he rather welcomed than otherwise the arrival of Marion Cavendish, who came a half-hour before Helen was expected, and who followed a hasty knock with a precipitate entrance.

"Sit down," she commanded breathlessly; "and listen. I've been at rehearsal all day, or I'd have been here before you were awake." She seated herself nervously and nodded her head at Carroll in an excited and mysterious manner.

"What is it?" he asked. "Have you and Reggie — "

"Listen," Marion repeated, "our fortunes are made; that is what's the matter — and I've made them. If you took half the interest in your work I do, you'd have made yours long ago. Last night," she began impressively, "I went to a large supper at the Savoy, and I sat next to Charley Wimpole. He came in late, after everybody had finished, and I attacked him while he was eating his supper. He said he had been rehearsing 'Caste' after the performance; that they've put it on as a stop-gap on account of the failure of the 'Triflers,' and that he knew revivals were of no use ; that he would give any sum for a good modern comedy. That was my cue, and I told him I knew of a better comedy than any he had produced at his theatre in five years, and that it was going begging. He laughed, and asked where was he to find this wonderful comedy, and I said,

' It 's been in your safe for the last two months and you have n't read it.' He said, ' Indeed, how do you know that?' and I said, 'Because if you 'd read it, it would n't be in your safe, but on your stage.' So he asked me what the play was about, and I told him the plot and what sort of a part his was, and some of his scenes, and he began to take notice. He forgot his supper, and very soon he grew so interested that he turned his chair round and kept eying my supper-card to find out who I was, and at last remembered seeing me in ' The New Boy ' — and a rotten part it was, too — but he remembered it, and he told me to go on and tell him more about your play. So I recited it, bit by bit, and he laughed in all the right places and got very much excited, and said finally that he would read it the first thing this morning." Marion paused, breathlessly. " Oh, yes, and he wrote your address on his cuff," she added, with the air of delivering a complete and convincing climax.

Carroll stared at her and pulled excitedly on his pipe.

" Oh, Marion ! " he gasped, " suppose he

53

The Lion and the Unicorn

should? He won't though," he added, but
eying her eagerly and inviting contradiction.

"He will," she answered, stoutly, "if he
reads it."

"The other managers read it," Carroll
suggested, doubtfully.

"Yes, but what do they know?" Marion
returned, loftily. "He knows. Charles
Wimpole is the only intelligent actor-manager in London."

There was a sharp knock at the door,
which Marion in her excitement had left ajar,
and Prentiss threw it wide open with an im-
pressive sweep, as though he were announc-
ing royalty: "Mr. Charles Wimpole," he
said.

The actor-manager stopped in the door-
way bowing gracefully, his hat held before
him and his hand on his stick as though it
were resting on a foil. He had the face and
carriage of a gallant of the days of Congreve,
and he wore his modern frock-coat with as
much distinction as if it were of silk and lace.
He was evidently amused. "I couldn't help
overhearing the last line," he said, smiling.
"It gives me a good entrance."

The Lion and the Unicorn

Marion gazed at him blankly: "Oh," she gasped, "we — we — were just talking about you."

"If you hadn't mentioned my name," the actor said, "I should never have guessed it. And this is Mr. Carroll, I hope."

The great man was rather pleased with the situation. As he read it, it struck him as possessing strong dramatic possibilities: Carroll was the struggling author on the verge of starvation: Marion, his sweetheart, flying to him gave him hope; and he was the good fairy arriving in the nick of time to set everything right and to make the young people happy and prosperous. He rather fancied himself in the part of the good fairy, and as he seated himself he bowed to them both in a manner which was charmingly inclusive and confidential.

"Miss Cavendish, I imagine, has already warned you that you might expect a visit from me," he said tentatively. Carroll nodded. He was too much concerned to interrupt.

"Then I need only tell you," Wimpole continued, "that I got up at an absurd hour

55

this morning to read your play; that I did read it; that I like it immensely — and that if we can come to terms I shall produce it. I shall produce it at once, within a fortnight or three weeks."

Carroll was staring at him intently and continued doing so after Wimpole had finished speaking. The actor felt he had somehow missed his point, or that Carroll could not have understood him, and repeated, " I say I shall put it in rehearsal at once."

Carroll rose abruptly, and pushed back his chair. " I should be very glad," he murmured, and strode over to the window, where he stood with his back turned to his guests. Wimpole looked after him with a kindly smile and nodded his head appreciatively. He had produced even a greater effect than his lines seemed to warrant. When he spoke again, it was quite simply, and sincerely, and though he spoke for Carroll's benefit, he addressed himself to Marion.

" You were quite right last night," he said, " it is a most charming piece of work. I am really extremely grateful to you for bringing it to my notice." He rose, and going to

Carroll, put his hand on his shoulder. "My boy," he said, "I congratulate you. I should like to be your age, and to have written that play. Come to my theatre to-morrow and we will talk terms. Talk it over first with your friends, so that I sha'n't rob you. Do you think you would prefer a lump sum now, and so be done with it altogether, or trust that the royalties may—"

"Royalties," prompted Marion, in an eager aside.

The men laughed. "Quite right," Wimpole assented, good-humoredly; "it's a poor sportsman who does n't back his own horse. Well, then, until to-morrow."

"But," Carroll began, "one moment please. I have n't thanked you."

"My dear boy," cried Wimpole, waving him away with his stick, "it is I who have to thank you."

"And—and there is a condition," Carroll said, "which goes with the play. It is that Miss Cavendish is to have the part of *Nancy*."

Wimpole looked serious and considered for a moment.

The Lion and the Unicorn

"*Nancy*," he said, "the girl who interferes — a very good part. I have cast Miss Maddox for it in my mind, but, of course, if the author insists — "

Marion, with her elbows on the table, clasped her hands appealingly before her.

" Oh, Mr. Wimpole!" she cried, "you owe me that, at least."

Carroll leaned over and took both of Marion's hands in one of his.

" It's all right," he said; " the author insists."

Wimpole waved his stick again as though it were the magic wand of the good fairy.

"You shall have it," he said. " I recall your performance in 'The New Boy' with pleasure. I take the play, and Miss Cavendish shall be cast for *Nancy*. We shall begin rehearsals at once. I hope you are a quick study."

" I 'm letter-perfect now " laughed Marion.

Wimpole turned at the door and nodded to them. They were both so young, so eager, and so jubilant that he felt strangely old and out of it. " Good-by, then," he said.

" Good-by, sir," they both chorussed.

The Lion and the Unicorn

And Marion cried after him, "And thank you a thousand times."

He turned again and looked back at them, but in their rejoicing they had already forgotten him. "Bless you, my children," he said, smiling. As he was about to close the door a young girl came down the passage toward it, and as she was apparently going to Carroll's rooms, the actor left the door open behind him.

Neither Marion nor Carroll had noticed his final exit. They were both gazing at each other as though, could they find speech, they would ask if it were true.

"It's come at last, Marion," Philip said, with an uncertain voice.

"I could weep," cried Marion. "Philip," she exclaimed, "I would rather see that play succeed than any play ever written, and I would rather play that part in it than — Oh, Philip," she ended. "I'm so proud of you!" and rising, she threw her arms about his neck and sobbed on his shoulder.

Carroll raised one of her hands and kissed the tips of her fingers gently. "I owe it to you, Marion," he said — "all to you."

The Lion and the Unicorn

This was the tableau that was presented
through the open door to Miss Helen Cabot,
hurrying on her errand of restitution and
good-will, and with Philip's ring and watch
clasped in her hand. They had not heard
her, nor did they see her at the door, so she
drew back quickly and ran along the passage
and down the stairs into the street.

She did not need now to analyze her feelings. They were only too evident. For she
could translate what she had just seen as
meaning only one thing — that she had considered Philip's love so lightly that she had
not felt it passing away from her until her
neglect had killed it — until it was too late.
And now that it was too late she felt that
without it her life could not go on. She tried
to assure herself that only the fact that she
had lost it made it seem invaluable, but this
thought did not comfort her — she was not
deceived by it, she knew that at last she cared
for him deeply and entirely. In her distress
she blamed herself bitterly, but she also
blamed Philip no less bitterly for having
failed to wait for her. "He might have
known that I must love him in time," she re-

peated to herself again and again. She was so unhappy that her letter congratulating Philip on his good fortune in having his comedy accepted seemed to him cold and unfeeling, and as his success meant for him only what it meant to her, he was hurt and grievously disappointed.

He accordingly turned the more readily to Marion, whose interests and enthusiasm at the rehearsals of the piece seemed in contrast most friendly and unselfish. He could not help but compare the attitude of the two girls at this time, when the failure or success of his best work was still undecided. He felt that as Helen took so little interest in his success he could not dare to trouble her with his anxieties concerning it, and she attributed his silence to his preoccupation and interest in Marion. So the two grew apart, each misunderstanding the other and each troubled in spirit at the other's indifference.

The first night of the play justified all that Marion and Wimpole had claimed for it, and was a great personal triumph for the new playwright. The audience was the typical first-night audience of the class which Charles Wimpole always commanded. It was brilliant, intelligent, and smart, and it came prepared to be pleased.

From one of the upper stage-boxes Helen and Lady Gower watched the successful progress of the play with an anxiety almost as keen as that of the author. To Helen it seemed as though the giving of these lines to the public — these lines which he had so often read to her, and altered to her liking — was a desecration. It seemed as though she were losing him indeed — as though he now belonged to these strange people, all of whom were laughing and applauding his words, from the German Princess in the Royal box to the straight-backed Tommy in the pit. Instead of the painted scene before her, she saw the birch-trees by the river at home, where he had first read her the speech to which they were now listening so intensely — the speech in which the hero tells the girl he loves her. She remembered that at the time she had thought how wonderful it would be if some day some one made such a speech to her — not Philip — but a man she loved.

62

And now? If Philip would only make that speech to her now!

He came out at last, with Wimpole leading him, and bowed across a glaring barrier of lights at a misty but vociferous audience that was shouting the generous English bravo! and standing up to applaud. He raised his eyes to the box where Helen sat, and saw her staring down at the tumult, with her hands clasped under her chin. Her face was colorless, but lit with the excitement of the moment; and he saw that she was crying.

Lady Gower, from behind her, was clapping her hands delightedly.

"But, my dear Helen," she remonstrated breathlessly, "you never told me he was so good-looking."

"Yes," said Helen, rising abruptly, "he is —very good-looking."

She crossed the box to where her cloak was hanging, but instead of taking it down buried her face in its folds.

"My dear child!" cried Lady Gower, in dismay. "What is it? The excitement has been too much for you."

The Lion and the Unicorn

" No, I am just happy," sobbed Helen. " I am just happy for him."

"We will go and tell him so then," said Lady Gower. " I am sure he would like to hear it from you to-night."

Philip was standing in the centre of the stage, surrounded by many pretty ladies and elderly men. Wimpole was hovering over him as though he had claims upon him by the right of discovery.

But when Philip saw Helen, he pushed his way toward her eagerly and took her hand in both of his.

" I am so glad, Phil," she said. She felt it all so deeply that she was afraid to say more, but that meant so much to her that she was sure he would understand.

He had planned it very differently. For a year he had dreamed that, on the first night of his play, there would be a supper, and that he would rise and drink her health, and tell his friends and the world that she was the woman he loved, and that she had agreed to marry him, and that at last he was able, through the success of his play, to make her his wife.

64

Saw her staring down at the tumult.

The Lion and the Unicorn

And now they met in a crowd to shake hands, and she went her way with one of her grand ladies, and he was left among a group of chattering strangers. The great English playwright took him by the hand and in the hearing of all, praised him gracefully and kindly. It did not matter to Philip whether the older playwright believed what he said or not; he knew it was generously meant.

"I envy you this," the great man was saying. "Don't lose any of it, stay and listen to all they have to say. You will never live through the first night of your first play but once."

"Yes, I hear them," said Philip, nervously; "they are all too kind. But I don't hear the voice I have been listening for," he added in a whisper. The older man pressed his hand again quickly. "My dear boy," he said, "I am sorry."

"Thank you," Philip answered.

Within a week he had forgotten the great man's fine words of praise, but the clasp of his hand he cherished always.

Helen met Marion as she was leaving the stage door and stopped to congratulate her

5   65

on her success in the new part. Marion was radiant. To Helen she seemed obstreperously happy and jubilant.

"And, Marion," Helen began bravely, "I also want to congratulate you on something else. You — you — neither of you have told me yet," she stammered, "but I am such an old friend of both that I will not be kept out of the secret." At these words Marion's air of triumphant gayety vanished; she regarded Helen's troubled eyes closely and kindly.

"What secret, Helen?" she asked.

"I came to the door of Philip's room the other day when you did not know I was there," Helen answered; "and I could not help seeing how matters were. And I do congratulate you both — and wish you — oh, such happiness!" Without a word Marion dragged her back down the passage to her dressing-room, and closed the door.

"Now tell me what you mean," she said.

"I am sorry if I discovered anything you didn't want known yet," said Helen, "but the door was open. Mr. Wimpole had just left you and had not shut it, and I could not help seeing."

Marion interrupted her with an eager exclamation of enlightenment.

"Oh, you were there, then," she cried. "And you?" she asked eagerly — "you thought Phil cared for me — that we are engaged, and it hurt you; you are sorry? Tell me," she demanded, "are you sorry?"

Helen drew back and stretched out her hand toward the door.

"How can you!" she exclaimed, indignantly. "You have no right."

Marion stood between her and the door.

"I have every right," she said, "to help my friends, and I want to help you and Philip. And indeed I do hope you *are* sorry. I hope you are miserable. And I'm glad you saw me kiss him. That was the first and the last time, and I did it because I was happy and glad for him; and because I love him too, but not in the least in the way he loves you. No one ever loved any one as he loves you. And it's time you found it out. And if I have helped to make you find it out I'm glad, and I don't care how much I hurt you."

"Marion!" exclaimed Helen, "what does

67

it mean? Do you mean that you are not engaged; that —"

"Certainly not," Marion answered. "I
am going to marry Reggie. It is you that
Philip loves, and I am very sorry for you that
you don't love him."

Helen clasped Marion's hands in both of
hers.

"But, Marion!" she cried, "I do, oh, I
do!"

There was a thick yellow fog the next
morning, and with it rain and a sticky, de-
pressing dampness which crept through the
window-panes, and which neither a fire nor
blazing gas-jets could overcome.

Philip stood in front of the fireplace with
the morning papers piled high on the centre-
table and scattered over the room about him.

He had read them all, and he knew now
what it was to wake up famous, but he could
not taste it. Now that it had come it meant
nothing, and that it was so complete a triumph only made it the harder. In his most
optimistic dreams he had never imagined
success so satisfying as the reality had proved

The Lion and the Unicorn

to be; but in his dreams Helen had always
held the chief part, and without her, success
seemed only to mock him.

He wanted to lay it all before her, to say,
"If you are pleased, I am happy. If you
are satisfied, then I am content. It was done
for you, and I am wholly yours, and all that
I do is yours." And, as though in answer
to his thoughts, there was an instant knock
at the door, and Helen entered the room
and stood smiling at him across the table.

Her eyes were lit with excitement, and
spoke with many emotions, and her cheeks
were brilliant with color. He had never seen
her look more beautiful.

"Why, Helen!" he exclaimed, "how good
of you to come. Is there anything wrong?
Is anything the matter?"

She tried to speak, but faltered, and smiled
at him appealingly.

"What is it?" he asked in great concern.

Helen drew in her breath quickly, and at
the same moment motioned him away — and
he stepped back and stood watching her in
much perplexity.

With her eyes fixed on his she raised her

hands to her head, and her fingers fumbled with the knot of her veil. She pulled it loose, and then, with a sudden courage, lifted her hat proudly, as though it were a coronet, and placed it between them on his table.

"Philip," she stammered, with the tears in her voice and eyes, "if you will let me — I have come to stay."

The table was no longer between them. He caught her in his arms and kissed her face and her uncovered head again and again. From outside the rain beat drearily and the fog rolled through the street, but inside before the fire the two young people sat close together, asking eager questions or sitting in silence, staring at the flames with wondering, happy eyes.

The Lion and the Unicorn saw them only once again. It was a month later when they stopped in front of the shop in a four-wheeler, with their baggage mixed on top of it, and steamer-labels pasted over every trunk.

"And, oh, Prentiss!" Carroll called from the cab-window. "I came near forgetting.

The Lion and the Unicorn

I promised to gild the Lion and the Unicorn if I won out in London. So have it done, please, and send the bill to me. For I 've won out all right." And then he shut the door of the cab, and they drove away forever.

"Nice gal, that," growled the Lion. "I always liked her. I am glad they 've settled it at last."

The Unicorn sighed, sentimentally. "The other one 's worth two of her," he said.

On the Fever Ship

THERE were four rails around the ship's
sides, the three lower ones of iron and
the one on top of wood, and as he looked
between them from the canvas cot he recognized them as the prison-bars which held him
in. Outside his prison lay a stretch of blinding
blue water which ended in a line of breakers
and a yellow coast with ragged palms. Beyond that again rose a range of mountain-
peaks, and, stuck upon the loftiest peak of all,
a tiny block-house. It rested on the brow of
the mountain against the naked sky as impu-
dently as a cracker-box set upon the dome of
a great cathedral.

As the transport rode on her anchor-chains,
the iron bars around her sides rose and sank
and divided the landscape with parallel lines.
From his cot the officer followed this phe-
nomenon with severe, painstaking interest.
Sometimes the wooden rail swept up to the

On the Fever Ship

very block-house itself, and for a second of
time blotted it from sight. And again it
sank to the level of the line of breakers, and
wiped them out of the picture as though they
were a line of chalk.

The soldier on the cot promised himself
that the next swell of the sea would send the
lowest rail climbing to the very top of the
palm-trees or, even higher, to the base of the
mountains ; and when it failed to reach even
the palm-trees he felt a distinct sense of ill use,
of having been wronged by some one. There
was no other reason for submitting to this
existence, save these tricks upon the weari-
some, glaring landscape ; and, now, whoever
it was who was working them did not seem
to be making this effort to entertain him with
any heartiness.

It was most cruel. Indeed, he decided
hotly, it was not to be endured; he would
bear it no longer, he would make his escape.
But he knew that this move, which could be
conceived in a moment's desperation, could
only be carried to success with great strategy,
secrecy, and careful cunning. So he fell
back upon his pillow and closed his eyes, as

though he were asleep, and then opening them again, turned cautiously, and spied upon his keeper. As usual, his keeper sat at the foot of the cot turning the pages of a huge paper filled with pictures of the war printed in daubs of tawdry colors. His keeper was a hard-faced boy without human pity or consideration, a very devil of obstinacy and fiendish cruelty. To make it worse, the fiend was a person without a collar, in a suit of soiled khaki, with a curious red cross bound by a safety-pin to his left arm. He was intent upon the paper in his hands; he was holding it between his eyes and his prisoner. His vigilance had relaxed, and the moment seemed propitious. With a sudden plunge of arms and legs, the prisoner swept the bed-sheet from him, and sprang at the wooden rail and grasped the iron stanchion beside it. He had his knee pressed against the top bar and his bare toes on the iron rail beneath it. Below him the blue water waited for him. It was cool and dark and gentle and deep. It would certainly put out the fire in his bones, he thought; it might even shut out the glare of the sun which scorched his eyeballs.

On the Fever Ship

But as he balanced for the leap, a swift weakness and nausea swept over him, a weight seized upon his body and limbs. He could not lift the lower foot from the iron rail, and he swayed dizzily and trembled. He trembled. He who had raced his men and beaten them up the hot hill to the trenches of San Juan. But now he was a baby in the hands of a giant, who caught him by the wrist and with an iron arm clasped him around his waist and pulled him down, and shouted, brutally, " Help, some of you 'se, quick ; he 's at it again. I can't hold him."

More giants grasped him by the arms and by the legs. One of them took the hand that clung to the stanchion in both of his, and pulled back the fingers one by one, saying, " Easy now, Lieutenant — easy."

The ragged palms and the sea and block-house were swallowed up in a black fog, and his body touched the canvas cot again with a sense of home-coming and relief and rest. He wondered how he could have cared to escape from it. He found it so good to be back again that for a long time he wept quite happily, until the fiery pillow was moist and cool.

On the Fever Ship

The world outside of the iron bars was like a scene in a theatre set for some great event, but the actors were never ready. He remembered confusedly a play he had once witnessed before that same scene. Indeed, he believed he had played some small part in it; but he remembered it dimly, and all trace of the men who had appeared with him in it was gone. He had reasoned it out that they were up there behind the range of mountains, because great heavy wagons and ambulances and cannon were emptied from the ships at the wharf above and were drawn away in long lines behind the ragged palms, moving always toward the passes between the peaks. At times he was disturbed by the thought that he should be up and after them, that some tradition of duty made his presence with them imperative. There was much to be done back of the mountains. Some event of momentous import was being carried forward there, in which he held a part; but the doubt soon passed from him, and he was content to lie and watch the iron bars rising and falling between the block-house and the white surf.

On the Fever Ship

If they had been only humanely kind, his lot would have been bearable, but they starved him and held him down when he wished to rise ; and they would not put out the fire in the pillow, which they might easily have done by the simple expedient of throwing it over the ship's side into the sea. He himself had done this twice, but the keeper had immediately brought a fresh pillow already heated for the torture and forced it under his head.

His pleasures were very simple, and so few that he could not understand why they robbed him of them so jealously. One was to watch a green cluster of bananas that hung above him from the awning twirling on a string. He could count as many of them as five before the bunch turned and swung lazily back again, when he could count as high as twelve; sometimes when the ship rolled heavily he could count to twenty. It was a most fascinating game, and contented him for many hours. But when they found this out they sent for the cook to come and cut them down, and the cook carried them away to his galley.

On the Fever Ship

Then, one day, a man came out from the shore, swimming through the blue water with great splashes. He was a most charming man, who spluttered and dove and twisted and lay on his back and kicked his legs in an excess of content and delight. It was a real pleasure to watch him; not for days had anything so amusing appeared on the other side of the prison-bars. But as soon as the keeper saw that the man in the water was amusing his prisoner, he leaned over the ship's side and shouted, " Sa-ay, you, don't you know there's sharks in there?"

And the swimming man said, "The h—ll there is!" and raced back to the shore like a porpoise with great lashing of the water, and ran up the beach half-way to the palms before he was satisfied to stop. Then the prisoner wept again. It was so disappointing. Life was robbed of everything now. He remembered that in a previous existence soldiers who cried were laughed at and mocked. But that was so far away and it was such an absurd superstition that he had no patience with it. For what could be more comforting to a man when he is treated

cruelly than to cry. It was so obvious an
exercise, and when one is so feeble that one
cannot vault a four-railed barrier it is something to feel that at least one is strong enough
to cry.

He escaped occasionally, traversing space
with marvellous rapidity and to great dis-
tances, but never to any successful purpose;
and his flight inevitably ended in ignominious
recapture and a sudden awakening in bed.
At these moments the familiar and hated
palms, the peaks and the block-house were
more hideous in their reality than the most
terrifying of his nightmares.

These excursions afield were always pre-
datory; he went forth always to seek food.
With all the beautiful world from which to
elect and choose, he sought out only those
places where eating was studied and elevated
to an art. These visits were much more
vivid in their detail than any he had ever
before made to these same resorts. They
invariably began in a carriage, which carried
him swiftly over smooth asphalt. One route
brought him across a great and beautiful
square, radiating with rows and rows of

flickering lights; two fountains splashed in the centre of the square, and six women of stone guarded its approaches. One of the women was hung with wreaths of mourning. Ahead of him the late twilight darkened behind a great arch, which seemed to rise on the horizon of the world, a great window into the heavens beyond. At either side strings of white and colored globes hung among the trees, and the sound of music came joyfully from theatres in the open air. He knew the restaurant under the trees to which he was now hastening, and the fountain beside it, and the very sparrows balancing on the fountain's edge; he knew every waiter at each of the tables, he felt again the gravel crunching under his feet, he saw the *maître d'hôtel* coming forward smiling to receive his command, and the waiter in the green apron bowing at his elbow, deferential and important, presenting the list of wines. But his adventure never passed that point, for he was captured again and once more bound to his cot with a close burning sheet.

Or else, he drove more sedately through

the London streets in the late evening twilight, leaning expectantly across the doors of the hansom and pulling carefully at his white gloves. Other hansoms flashed past him, the occupant of each with his mind fixed on one idea — dinner. He was one of a million of people who were about to dine, or who had dined, or who were deep in dining. He was so famished, so weak for food of any quality, that the galloping horse in the hansom seemed to crawl. The lights of the Embankment passed like the lamps of a railroad station as seen from the window of an express; and while his mind was still torn between the choice of a thin or thick soup or an immediate attack upon cold beef, he was at the door, and the *chasseur* touched his cap, and the little *chasseur* put the wicker guard over the hansom's wheel. As he jumped out he said, "Give him half-a-crown," and the driver called after him, "Thank you, sir."

It was a beautiful world, this world outside of the iron bars. Every one in it contributed to his pleasure and to his comfort. In this world he was not starved nor man-

handled. He thought of this joyfully as he
leaped up the stairs, where young men with
grave faces and with their hands held negli-
gently behind their backs bowed to him in
polite surprise at his speed. But they had
not been starved on condensed milk. He
threw his coat and hat at one of them, and
came down the hall fearfully and quite weak
with dread lest it should not be real. His
voice was shaking when he asked Ellis if he
had reserved a table. The place was all so
real, it must be true this time. The way
Ellis turned and ran his finger down the list
showed it was real, because Ellis always did
that, even when he knew there would not be
an empty table for an hour. The room was
crowded with beautiful women; under the
light of the red shades they looked kind and
approachable, and there was food on every
table, and iced drinks in silver buckets. It
was with the joy of great relief that he heard
Ellis say to his underling, " Numéro cinq,
sur la terrace, un couvert." It was real at
last. Outside, the Thames lay a great gray
shadow. The lights of the Embankment
flashed and twinkled across it, the tower of

the House of Commons rose against the sky, and here, inside, the waiter was hurrying toward him carrying a smoking plate of rich soup with a pungent intoxicating odor.

And then the ragged palms, the glaring sun, the immovable peaks, and the white surf stood again before him. The iron rails swept up and sank again, the fever sucked at his bones, and the pillow scorched his cheek.

One morning for a brief moment he came back to real life again and lay quite still, seeing everything about him with clear eyes and for the first time, as though he had but just that instant been lifted over the ship's side. His keeper, glancing up, found the prisoner's eyes considering him curiously, and recognized the change. The instinct of discipline brought him to his feet with his fingers at his sides.

" Is the Lieutenant feeling better? "

The Lieutenant surveyed him gravely.

" You are one of our hospital stewards."

" Yes, Lieutenant."

" Why ar' n't you with the regiment ? "

" I was wounded, too, sir. I got it same time you did, Lieutenant."

83

On the Fever Ship

"Am I wounded? Of course, I remember. Is this a hospital ship?"

The steward shrugged his shoulders. "She's one of the transports. They have turned her over to the fever cases."

The Lieutenant opened his lips to ask another question; but his own body answered that one, and for a moment he lay silent.

"Do they know up North that I — that I'm all right?"

"Oh, yes, the papers had it in — there was pictures of the Lieutenant in some of them."

"Then I've been ill some time?"

"Oh, about eight days."

The soldier moved uneasily, and the nurse in him became uppermost.

"I guess the Lieutenant had n't better talk any more," he said. It was his voice now which held authority.

The Lieutenant looked out at the palms and the silent gloomy mountains and the empty coast-line, where the same wave was rising and falling with weary persistence.

"Eight days," he said. His eyes shut quickly, as though with a sudden touch of pain. He turned his head and sought for the figure at the foot of the cot. Already the figure had grown faint and was receding and swaying.

"Has any one written or cabled?" the Lieutenant spoke, hurriedly. He was fearful lest the figure should disappear altogether before he could obtain his answer. "Has any one come?"

"Why, they could n't get here, Lieutenant, not yet."

The voice came very faintly. "You go to sleep now, and I 'll run and fetch some letters and telegrams. When you wake up, may be I 'll have a lot for you."

But the Lieutenant caught the nurse by the wrist, and crushed his hand in his own thin fingers. They were hot, and left the steward's skin wet with perspiration. The Lieutenant laughed gayly.

"You see, Doctor," he said, briskly, "that you can't kill me. I can't die. I 've got to live, you understand. Because, sir, she said she would come. She said if I was wounded, or if I was ill, she would come to me. She did n't care what people thought. She would

come any way and nurse me — well, she will
come.

"So, Doctor — old man — " He plucked
at the steward's sleeve, and stroked his hand
eagerly, "old man — " he began again, be-
seechingly, "you 'll not let me die until she
comes, will you? What? No, I know I won't
die. Nothing made by man can kill me.
No, not until she comes. Then, after that —
eight days, she 'll be here soon, any moment?
What? You think so, too? Don't you?
Surely, yes, any moment. Yes, I 'll go to
sleep now, and when you see her rowing out
from shore you wake me. You 'll know her;
you can't make a mistake. She is like — no,
there is no one like her — but you can't make
a mistake."

That day strange figures began to mount
the sides of the ship, and to occupy its every
turn and angle of space. Some of them fell
on their knees and slapped the bare deck
with their hands, and laughed and cried out,
"Thank God, I 'll see God's country again!"
Some of them were regulars, bound in ban-
dages; some were volunteers, dirty and hol-
low-eyed, with long beards on boys' faces.

On the Fever Ship

Some came on crutches; others with their arms around the shoulders of their comrades, staring ahead of them with a fixed smile, their lips drawn back and their teeth protruding. At every second step they stumbled, and the face of each was swept by swift ripples of pain.

They lay on cots so close together that the nurses could not walk between them. They lay on the wet decks, in the scuppers, and along the transoms and hatches. They were like shipwrecked mariners clinging to a raft, and they asked nothing more than that the ship's bow be turned toward home. Once satisfied as to that, they relaxed into a state of self-pity and miserable oblivion to their environment, from which hunger nor nausea nor aching bones could shake them.

The hospital steward touched the Lieutenant lightly on the shoulder.

"We are going North, sir," he said. "The transport's ordered North to New York, with these volunteers and the sick and wounded. Do you hear me, sir?"

The Lieutenant opened his eyes. "Has she come?" he asked.

On the Fever Ship

"Gee!" exclaimed the hospital steward. He glanced impatiently at the blue mountains and the yellow coast, from which the transport was drawing rapidly away.

"Well, I can't see her coming just now," he said. "But she will," he added.

"You let me know at once when she comes."

"Why, cert'nly, of course," said the steward.

Three trained nurses came over the side just before the transport started North. One was a large, motherly-looking woman, with a German accent. She had been a trained nurse, first in Berlin, and later in the London Hospital in Whitechapel, and at Bellevue. The nurse was dressed in white, and wore a little silver medal at her throat; and she was strong enough to lift a volunteer out of his cot and hold him easily in her arms, while one of the convalescents pulled his cot out of the rain. Some of the men called her "nurse;" others, who wore scapulars around their necks, called her "Sister;" and the officers of the medical staff addressed her as Miss Bergen.

Miss Bergen halted beside the cot of the

On the Fever Ship

Lieutenant and asked, "Is this the fever case you spoke about, Doctor — the one you want moved to the officers' ward?" She slipped her hand up under his sleeve and felt his wrist.

"His pulse is very high," she said to the steward. "When did you take his temperature?" She drew a little morocco case from her pocket and from that took a clinical thermometer, which she shook up and down, eying the patient meanwhile with a calm, impersonal scrutiny. The Lieutenant raised his head and stared up at the white figure beside his cot. His eyes opened and then shut quickly, with a startled look, in which doubt struggled with wonderful happiness. His hand stole out fearfully and warily until it touched her apron, and then, finding it was real, he clutched it desperately, and twisting his face and body toward her, pulled her down, clasping her hands in both of his, and pressing them close to his face and eyes and lips. He put them from him for an instant, and looked at her through his tears.

"Sweetheart," he whispered, "sweetheart, I knew you'd come."

As the nurse knelt on the deck beside him,

her thermometer slipped from her fingers and broke, and she gave an exclamation of annoyance. The young Doctor picked up the pieces and tossed them overboard. Neither of them spoke, but they smiled appreciatively. The Lieutenant was looking at the nurse with the wonder and hope and hunger of soul in his eyes with which a dying man looks at the cross the priest holds up before him. What he saw where the German nurse was kneeling was a tall, fair girl with great bands and masses of hair, with a head rising like a lily from a firm, white throat, set on broad shoulders above a straight back and sloping breast — a tall, beautiful creature, half-girl, half-woman, who looked back at him shyly, but steadily.

" Listen," he said.

The voice of the sick man was so sure and so sane that the young Doctor started, and moved nearer to the head of the cot. " Listen, dearest," the Lieutenant whispered. " I wanted to tell you before I came South. But I did not dare ; and then I was afraid something might happen to me, and I could never tell you, and you would never know. So I

" Listen," he said.

wrote it to you in the will I made at Baiquiri, the night before the landing. If you had n't come now, you would have learned it in that way. You would have read there that there never was any one but you ; the rest were all dream people, foolish, silly — mad. There is no one else in the world but you; you have been the only thing in life that has counted. I thought I might do something down here that would make you care. But I got shot going up a hill, and after that I was n't able to do anything. It was very hot, and the hills were on fire ; and they took me prisoner, and kept me tied down here, burning on these coals. I can't live much longer, but now that I have told you I can have peace. They tried to kill me before you came ; but they did n't know I loved you, they did n't know that men who love you can't die. They tried to starve my love for you, to burn it out of me ; they tried to reach it with their knives. But my love for you is my soul, and they can't kill a man's soul. Dear heart, I have lived because you lived. Now that you know — now that you understand — what does it matter? "

On the Fever Ship

Miss Bergen shook her head with great vigor. "Nonsense," she said, cheerfully. "You are not going to die. As soon as we move you out of this rain, and some food cook —"

"Good God!" cried the young Doctor, savagely. "Do you want to kill him?"

When she spoke the patient had thrown his arms heavily across his face, and had fallen back, lying rigid on the pillow.

The Doctor led the way across the prostrate bodies, apologizing as he went. "I am sorry I spoke so quickly," he said, "but he thought you were real. I mean he thought you were some one he really knew—"

"He was just delirious," said the German nurse, calmly.

The Doctor mixed himself a Scotch and soda and drank it with a single gesture.

"Ugh!" he said to the ward-room. "I feel as though I'd been opening another man's letters."

The transport drove through the empty seas with heavy, clumsy upheavals, rolling like a buoy. Having been originally intended for the freight-carrying trade, she had no sympathy with hearts that beat for a sight of their native land, or for lives that counted their remaining minutes by the throbbing of her engines. Occasionally, without apparent reason, she was thrown violently from her course: but it was invariably the case that when her stern went to starboard, something splashed in the water on her port side and drifted past her, until, when it had cleared the blades of her propeller, a voice cried out, and she was swung back on her home-bound track again.

The Lieutenant missed the familiar palms and the tiny block-house; and seeing nothing beyond the iron rails but great wastes of gray water, he decided he was on board a prison-ship, or that he had been strapped to a raft and cast adrift. People came for hours at a time and stood at the foot of his cot, and talked with him and he to them — people he had loved and people he had long forgotten, some of whom he had thought were dead. One of them he could have sworn he had seen buried in a deep trench, and covered with branches of palmetto. He had heard the bugler, with tears choking him, sound "taps;" and with his own hand he had placed the dead man's campaign hat on the mound of fresh earth above the grave. Yet here he was still alive, and he came with other men of his troop to speak to him ; but when he reached out to them they were gone — the real and the unreal, the dead and the living — and even She disappeared whenever he tried to take her hand, and sometimes the hospital steward drove her away.

"Did that young lady say when she was coming back again?" he asked the steward.

"The young lady! What young lady?" asked the steward, wearily.

"The one who has been sitting there," he answered. He pointed with his gaunt hand at the man in the next cot.

"Oh, that young lady. Yes, she's coming back. She's just gone below to fetch you some hard-tack."

The young volunteer in the next cot whined grievously.

"That crazy man gives me the creeps," he groaned. " He's always waking me up, and looking at me as though he was going to eat me."

"Shut your head," said the steward. "He's a better man crazy than you'll ever be with the little sense you've got. And he has two Mauser holes in him. Crazy, eh? It's a damned good thing for you that there was about four thousand of us regulars just as crazy as him, or you'd never seen the top of the hill."

One morning there was a great commotion on deck, and all the convalescents balanced themselves on the rail, shivering in their pajamas, and pointed one way. The transport was moving swiftly and smoothly through water as flat as a lake, and making a great noise with her steam-whistle. The noise was echoed by many more steam-whistles ; and the ghosts of out-bound ships and tugs and excursion steamers ran past her out of the mist and disappeared, saluting joyously. All of the excursion steamers had a heavy list to the side nearest the transport, and the ghosts on them crowded to that rail and waved handkerchiefs and cheered. The fog lifted suddenly, and between the iron

rails the Lieutenant saw high green hills on
either side of a great harbor. Houses and
trees and thousands of masts swept past like
a panorama; and beyond was a mirage of
three cities, with curling smoke-wreaths and
sky-reaching buildings, and a great swinging
bridge, and a giant statue of a woman waving a welcome home.

The Lieutenant surveyed the spectacle with
cynical disbelief. He was far too wise and
far too cunning to be bewitched by it. In
his heart he pitied the men about him, who
laughed wildly, and shouted, and climbed
recklessly to the rails and ratlines. He had
been deceived too often not to know that it
was not real. He knew from cruel experience that in a few moments the tall buildings
would crumble away, the thousands of columns of white smoke that flashed like snow
in the sun, the busy, shrieking tug-boats, and
the great statue would vanish into the sea,
leaving it gray and bare. He closed his eyes
and shut the vision out. It was so beautiful
that it tempted him; but he would not be
mocked, and he buried his face in his hands.
They were carrying the farce too far, he

thought. It was really too absurd; for now they were at a wharf which was so real that, had he not known by previous suffering, he would have been utterly deceived by it. And there were great crowds of smiling, cheering people, and a waiting guard of honor in fresh uniforms, and rows of police pushing the people this way and that; and these men about him were taking it all quite seriously, and making ready to disembark, carrying their blanket-rolls and rifles with them.

A band was playing joyously, and the man in the next cot, who was being lifted to a stretcher, said, "There's the Governor and his staff; that's him in the high hat." It was really very well done. The Custom-house and the Elevated Railroad and Castle Garden were as like to life as a photograph, and the crowd was as well handled as a mob in a play. His heart ached for it so that he could not bear the pain, and he turned his back on it. It was cruel to keep it up so long. His keeper lifted him in his arms, and pulled him into a dirty uniform which had belonged, apparently, to a much larger man — a man who had been killed probably, for there were

7   97

dark-brown marks of blood on the tunic and breeches. When he tried to stand on his feet, Castle Garden and the Battery disappeared in a black cloud of night, just as he knew they would; but when he opened his eyes from the stretcher, they had returned again. It was a most remarkably vivid vision. They kept it up so well. Now the young Doctor and the hospital steward were pretending to carry him down a gang-plank and into an open space; and he saw quite close to him a long line of policemen, and behind them thousands of faces, some of them women's faces — women who pointed at him and then shook their heads and cried, and pressed their hands to their cheeks, still looking at him. He wondered why they cried. He did not know them, nor did they know him. No one knew him; these people were only ghosts.

There was a quick parting in the crowd. A man he had once known shoved two of the policemen to one side, and he heard a girl's voice speaking his name, like a sob; and She came running out across the open space and fell on her knees beside the stretcher, and bent down over him, and he was clasped in two young, firm arms.

"Of course it is not real, of course it is not She," he assured himself. "Because She would not do such a thing. Before all these people She would not do it."

But he trembled and his heart throbbed so cruelly that he could not bear the pain.

She was pretending to cry.

"They wired us you had started for Tampa on the hospital ship," She was saying, "and Aunt and I went all the way there before we heard you had been sent North. We have been on the cars a week. That is why I missed you. Do you understand? It was not my fault. I tried to come. Indeed, I tried to come."

She turned her head and looked up fearfully at the young Doctor.

"Tell me, why does he look at me like that?" she asked. "He does n't know me. Is he very ill? Tell me the truth." She drew in her breath quickly. "Of course you will tell me the truth."

When she asked the question he felt her arms draw tight about his shoulders. It was as though she was holding him to herself, and from some one who had reached out for him. In his trouble he turned to his old friend and keeper. His voice was hoarse and very low.

" Is this the same young lady who was on the transport — the one you used to drive away ? "

In his embarrassment, the hospital steward blushed under his tan, and stammered.

"Of course it's the same young lady," the Doctor answered briskly. " And I won't let them drive her away." He turned to her, smiling gravely. " I think his condition has ceased to be dangerous, madam," he said.

People who in a former existence had been his friends, and Her brother, gathered about his stretcher and bore him through the crowd and lifted him into a carriage filled with cushions, among which he sank lower and lower. Then She sat beside him, and he heard Her brother say to the coachman, " Home, and drive slowly and keep on the asphalt."

The carriage moved forward, and She put her arm about him and his head fell on her shoulder, and neither of them spoke. The vision had lasted so long now that he was torn with the joy that after all it might be real. But he could not bear the awakening if it were not, so he raised his head fearfully and looked up into the beautiful eyes above him. His brows were knit, and he struggled with a great doubt and an awful joy.

"Dearest," he said, " is it real?"

" Is it real?" she repeated.

Even as a dream, it was so wonderfully beautiful that he was satisfied if it could only continue so, if but for a little while.

" Do you think," he begged again, trembling, " that it is going to last much longer?"

She smiled, and, bending her head slowly, kissed him.

" It is going to last — always," she said.

The

Man with One Talent

THE mass-meeting in the Madison Square
Garden which was to help set Cuba
free was finished, and the people were pushing their way out of the overheated building
into the snow and sleet of the streets. They
had been greatly stirred and the spell of the
last speaker still hung so heavily upon them
that as they pressed down the long corridor
they were still speaking loudly in his praise.

A young man moved eagerly amongst
them, and pushed his way to wherever a
voice was raised above the rest. He strained
forward, listening openly, as though he tried
to judge the effect of the meeting by the ver-
dict of those about him.

But the words he overheard seemed to
clash with what he wished them to be, and
the eager look on his face changed to one of

doubt and of grave disappointment. When he had reached the sidewalk he stopped and stood looking back alternately into the lighted hall and at the hurrying crowds which were dispersing rapidly. He made a movement as though he would recall them, as though he felt they were still unconvinced, as though there was much still left unsaid.

A fat stranger halted at his elbow to light his cigar, and glancing up nodded his head approvingly.

"Fine speaker, Senator Stanton, ain't he?" he said.

The young man answered eagerly. "Yes," he assented, "he is a great orator, but how could he help but speak well with such a subject?"

"Oh, you ought to have heard him last November at Tammany Hall," the fat stranger answered. "He wasn't quite up to himself to-night. He wasn't so interested. Those Cubans are foreigners, you see, but you ought to heard him last St. Patrick's day on Home Rule for Ireland. Then he was talking! That speech made him a United States senator, I guess. I don't just see how he expects to win out on this Cuba game. The Cubans have n't got no votes."

The young man opened his eyes in some bewilderment.

"He speaks for the good of Cuba, for the sake of humanity," he ventured.

"What?" inquired the fat stranger. "Oh, yes, of course. Well, I must be getting on. Good-night, sir."

The stranger moved on his way, but the young man still lingered uncertainly in the snow-swept corridor shivering violently with the cold and stamping his feet for greater comfort. His face was burned to a deep red, which seemed to have come from some long exposure to a tropical sun, but which held no sign of health. His cheeks were hollow and his eyes were lighted with the fire of fever and from time to time he was shaken by violent bursts of coughing which caused him to reach toward one of the pillars for support.

As the last of the lights went out in the Garden, the speaker of the evening and three of his friends came laughing and talking down the long corridor. Senator Stanton was a conspicuous figure at any time, and even in those places where his portraits had not penetrated he was at once recognized as a personage. Something in his erect carriage and an unusual grace of movement, and the power and success in his face, made men turn to look at him. He had been told that he resembled the early portraits of Henry Clay, and he had never quite forgotten the coincidence.

The senator was wrapping the collar of his fur coat around his throat and puffing contentedly at a fresh cigar, and as he passed, the night watchman and the ushers bowed to the great man and stood looking after him with the half-humorous, half-envious deference that the American voter pays to the successful politician. At the sidewalk, the policemen hurried to open the door of his carriage and in their eagerness made a double line, through which he passed nodding to them gravely. The young man who had stood so long in waiting pushed his way through the line to his side.

"Senator Stanton," he began timidly, "might I speak to you a moment? My name is Arkwright; I am just back from Cuba, and I want to thank you for your speech. I am an American, and I thank God that I am since you are too, sir. No one has said anything since the war began that compares with what you said to-night. You put it nobly, and I know, for I've been there for three years, only I can't make other people understand it, and I am thankful that some one can. You'll forgive my stopping you, sir, but I wanted to thank you. I feel it very much."

Senator Stanton's friends had already seated themselves in his carriage and were looking out of the door and smiling with mock patience. But the senator made no move to follow them. Though they were his admirers they were sometimes skeptical, and he was not sorry that they should hear this uninvited tribute. So he made a pretence of buttoning his long coat about him, and nodded encouragingly to Arkwright to continue. "I'm glad you liked it, sir," he said with the pleasant, gracious smile that had won him a friend wherever it had won him a vote. "It is very satisfactory to know from one who is well informed on the subject that what I have said is correct. The situation there is truly terrible. You have just returned, you say? Where were you — in Havana?"

"No, in the other provinces, sir," Arkwright answered. "I have been all over the island, I am a civil engineer. The truth has not been half told about Cuba, I assure you, sir. It is massacre there, not war. It is partly so through ignorance, but nevertheless it is massacre. And what makes it worse is, that it is the massacre of the innocents. That is what I liked best of what you said in that great speech, the part about the women and children."

He reached out his hands detainingly, and then drew back as though in apology for having already kept the great man so long waiting in the cold. "I wish I could tell you some of the terrible things I have seen," he began again, eagerly, as Stanton made no movement to depart. "They are much worse than those you instanced to-night, and you could make so much better use of them than any one else. I have seen starving women nursing dead babies, and sometimes starving babies sucking their dead mother's breasts ; I have seen men cut down in the open roads and while digging in the fields — and two hundred women imprisoned in one room without food and eaten with small-pox, and huts burned while the people in them slept — "

The young man had been speaking impetuously, but he stopped as suddenly, for the senator was not listening to him. He had lowered his eyes and was looking with a glance of mingled fascination and disgust at Arkwright's hands. In his earnestness the young man had stretched them out, and as they showed behind the line of his ragged sleeves the others could see, even in the blurred light and falling snow, that the wrists of each hand were gashed and cut in dark-brown lines like the skin of a mulatto, and in places were a raw red, where the fresh skin had but just closed over. The young man paused and stood shivering, still holding his hands out rigidly before him.

The senator raised his eyes slowly and drew away.

The Man with One Talent

"What is that?" he said in a low voice, pointing with a gloved finger at the black lines on the wrists.

A sergeant in the group of policemen who had closed around the speakers answered him promptly from his profound fund of professional knowledge.

"That's handcuffs, senator," he said importantly, and glanced at Stanton as though to signify that at a word from him he would take this suspicious character into custody. The young man pulled the frayed cuffs of his shirt over his wrists and tucked his hands, which the cold had frozen into an ashy blue, under his armpits to warm them.

"No, they don't use handcuffs in the field," he said in the same low, eager tone; "they use ropes and leather thongs; they fastened me behind a horse and when he stumbled going down the trail it jerked me forward and the cords would tighten and tear the flesh. But they have had a long time to heal now. I have been eight months in prison."

The young men at the carriage window had ceased smiling and were listening intently. One of them stepped out and stood beside the carriage door looking down at the shivering figure before him with a close and curious scrutiny.

"Eight months in prison!" echoed the police sergeant with a note of triumph; "what did I tell you?"

"Hold your tongue!" said the young man at the carriage door. There was silence for a moment, while the men looked at the senator, as though waiting for him to speak.

"Where were you in prison, Mr. Arkwright?" he asked.

"First in the calaboose at Santa Clara for two months, and then in Cabañas. The Cubans who were taken when I was, were shot by the fusillade on different days during this last month. Two of them, the Ezetas, were father and son, and the Volunteer band played all the time the execution was going on, so that the other prisoners might not hear them cry 'Cuba Libre' when the order came to fire. But we heard them."

The senator shivered slightly and pulled his fur collar up farther around his face. "I'd like to talk with you," he said, "if you have nothing to do to-morrow. I'd like to go into this thing thoroughly. Congress must be made to take some action."

The young man clasped his hands eagerly. "Ah, Mr. Stanton, if you would," he cried, "if you would only give me an hour! I could tell you so much that you could use. And you can believe what I say, sir — it is not necessary to lie — God knows the truth is bad enough. I can give you names and dates for everything I say. Or I can do better than that, sir. I can take you there yourself — in three months I can show you all you need to see, without danger to you in any way. And they would not know me, now that I have grown a beard, and I am a skeleton to what I was. I can speak the language well, and I know just what you should see, and then you could come back as one speaking with authority and not have to say, 'I have read,' or 'have been told,' but you can say, 'These are the things I have seen' — and you could free Cuba."

The senator coughed and put the question aside for the moment with a wave of the hand that held his cigar. "We will talk of that to-morrow also. Come to lunch with me at one. My apartments are in the Berkeley on Fifth Avenue. But are n't you afraid to go back there?" he asked curiously. "I should think you 'd had enough of it. And you 've got a touch of fever, have n't you?" He leaned forward and peered into the other's eyes.

"It is only the prison fever," the young man answered; "food and this cold will drive that out of me. And I must go back. There is so much to do there," he added. "Ah, if I could tell them, as you can tell them, what I feel here." He struck his chest sharply with his hand, and on the instant fell into a fit of coughing so violent that the young man at the carriage door caught him around the waist, and one of the policemen supported him from the other side.

"You need a doctor," said the senator kindly. "I 'll ask mine to have a look at you. Don't forget, then, at one o'clock to-morrow. We will go into this thing thoroughly." He shook Arkwright warmly by the hand and stooping stepped into the carriage. The young man who had stood at the door followed him and crowded back

luxuriously against the cushions. The foot-
man swung himself up beside the driver, and
said "Uptown Delmonico's," as he wrapped
the fur rug around his legs, and with a salute
from the policemen and a scraping of hoofs
on the slippery asphalt the great man was
gone.

"That poor fellow needs a doctor," he said
as the carriage rolled up the avenue, "and
he needs an overcoat, and he needs food.
He needs about almost everything, by the
looks of him."

But the voice of the young man in the
corner of the carriage objected drowsily —

"On the contrary," he said, "it seemed to
me that he had the one thing needful."

By one o'clock of the day following, Senator Stanton, having read the reports of his
speech in the morning papers, punctuated
with "Cheers," "Tremendous enthusiasm"
and more "Cheers," was still in a willing
frame of mind toward Cuba and her self-
appointed envoy, young Mr. Arkwright.

Over night he had had doubts but that the
young man's enthusiasm would bore him on
the morrow, but Mr. Arkwright, when he

appeared, developed, on the contrary, a practical turn of mind which rendered his suggestions both flattering and feasible. He was still terribly in earnest, but he was clever enough or serious enough to see that the motives which appealed to him might not have sufficient force to move a successful statesman into action. So he placed before the senator only those arguments and reasons which he guessed were the best adapted to secure his interest and his help. His proposal as he set it forth was simplicity itself.

"Here is a map of the island," he said; "on it I have marked the places you can visit in safety, and where you will meet the people you ought to see. If you leave New York at midnight you can reach Tampa on the second day. From Tampa we cross in another day to Havana. There you can visit the Americans imprisoned in Morro and Cabañas, and in the streets you can see the starving pacificos. From Havana I shall take you by rail to Jucaro, Matanzas, Santa Clara and Cienfuegos. You will not be able to see the insurgents in the fields — it is not necessary that you should — but you can visit one of the sugar plantations and some of the insurgent chiefs will run the forts by night and come in to talk with you. I will show you burning fields and houses, and starving men and women by the thousands, and men and women dying of fevers. You can see Cuban prisoners shot by a firing squad and you can note how these rebels meet death. You can see all this in three weeks and be back in New York in a month, as any one can see it who wishes to learn the truth. Why, English members of Parliament go all the way to India and British Columbia to inform themselves about those countries, they travel thousands of miles, but only one member of either of our houses of Congress has taken the trouble to cross these eighty miles of water that lie between us and Cuba. You can either go quietly and incognito, as it were, or you can advertise the fact of your going, which would be better. And from the moment you start the interest in your visit will grow and increase until there will be no topic discussed in any of our papers except yourself, and what you are doing and what you mean to do.

The Man with One Talent

"By the time you return the people will be waiting, ready and eager to hear whatever you may have to say. Your word will be the last word for them. It is not as though you were some demagogue seeking notoriety, or a hotel piazza correspondent at Key West or Jacksonville. You are the only statesman we have, the only orator Americans will listen to, and I tell you that when you come before them and bring home to them as only you can the horrors of this war, you will be the only man in this country. You will be the Patrick Henry of Cuba; you can go down to history as the man who added the most beautiful island in the seas to the territory of the United States, who saved thousands of innocent children and women, and who dared to do what no other politician has dared to do — to go and see for himself and to come back and speak the truth. It only means a month out of your life, a month's trouble and discomfort, but with no risk. What is a month out of a lifetime, when that month means immortality to you and life to thousands? In a month you would make a half dozen after-dinner speeches and cause your friends to laugh and applaud. Why not wring their hearts instead, and hold this thing up before them as it is, and shake it in their faces? Show it to them in all its horror — bleeding, diseased and naked, an offence to our humanity, and to our prated love of liberty, and to our God."

The young man threw himself eagerly forward and beat the map with his open palm. But the senator sat apparently unmoved gazing thoughtfully into the open fire, and shook his head.

While the luncheon was in progress the young gentleman who the night before had left the carriage and stood at Arkwright's side, had entered the room and was listening intently. He had invited himself to some fresh coffee, and had then relapsed into an attentive silence, following what the others said with an amused and interested countenance. Stanton had introduced him as Mr. Livingstone, and appeared to take it for granted that Arkwright would know who he was. He seemed to regard him with a certain deference which Arkwright judged was due to some fixed position the young man held, either of social or of political value.

"I do not know," said Stanton with consideration, "that I am prepared to advocate the annexation of the island. It is a serious problem."

"I am not urging that," Arkwright interrupted anxiously; "the Cubans themselves do not agree as to that, and in any event it is an afterthought. Our object now should be to prevent further bloodshed. If you see a man beating a boy to death, you first save the boy's life and decide afterward where he is to go to school. If there were any one else, senator," Arkwright continued earnestly, "I would not trouble you. But we all know your strength in this country. You are independent and fearless, and men of both parties listen to you. Surely, God has given you this great gift of oratory, if you will forgive my speaking so, to use only in a great cause. A grand organ in a cathedral is placed there to lift men's thoughts to high resolves and purposes, not to make people dance. A street organ can do that. Now, here is a cause worthy of your great talents, worthy of a Daniel Webster, of a Henry Clay."

The senator frowned at the fire and shook his head doubtfully.

" If they knew what I was down there for," he asked, " would n't they put me in prison too? "

Arkwright laughed incredulously.

" Certainly not," he said; " you would go there as a private citizen, as a tourist to look on and observe. Spain is not seeking complications of that sort. She has troubles enough without imprisoning United States senators."

" Yes; but these fevers now," persisted Stanton, " they 're no respecter of persons, I imagine. A United States senator is not above smallpox or cholera."

Arkwright shook his head impatiently and sighed.

" It is difficult to make it clear to one who has not been there," he said. " These people and soldiers are dying of fever because they are forced to live like pigs, and they are already sick with starvation. A healthy man like yourself would be in no more danger than you would be in walking through the wards of a New York hospital."

Senator Stanton turned in his armchair, and held up his hand impressively.

" If I were to tell them the things you have told me," he said warningly, " if I were to say I have seen such things — American property in flames, American interests ruined, and that five times as many women and children have died of fever and starvation in three months in Cuba as the Sultan has massacred in Armenia in three years — it would mean war with Spain."

" Well? " said Arkwright.

Stanton shrugged his shoulders and sank back again in his chair.

" It would either mean war," Arkwright went on, "or it might mean the sending of the Red Cross army to Cuba. It went to Constantinople, five thousand miles away, to help the Armenian Christians — why has it waited three years to go eighty miles to feed and clothe the Cuban women and children? It is like sending help to a hungry peasant in Russia while a man dies on your doorstep."

The Man with One Talent

"Well," said the senator, rising, "I will let you know to-morrow. If it is the right thing to do, and if I can do it, of course it must be done. We start from Tampa, you say? I know the presidents of all of those roads and they'll probably give me a private car for the trip down. Shall we take any newspaper men with us, or shall I wait until I get back and be interviewed? What do you think?"

"I would wait until my return," Arkwright answered, his eyes glowing with the hope the senator's words had inspired, "and then speak to a mass-meeting here and in Boston and in Chicago. Three speeches will be enough. Before you have finished your last one the American warships will be in the harbor of Havana."

"Ah, youth, youth!" said the senator, smiling gravely, "it is no light responsibility to urge a country into war."

"It is no light responsibility," Arkwright answered, "to know you have the chance to save the lives of thousands of little children and helpless women and to let the chance pass."

The Man with One Talent

"Quite so, that is quite true," said the senator. "Well, good-morning. I shall let you know to-morrow."

Young Livingstone went down in the elevator with Arkwright, and when they had reached the sidewalk stood regarding him for a moment in silence.

"You must n't count too much on Stanton, you know," he said kindly; "he has a way of disappointing people."

"Ah, he can never disappoint me," Arkwright answered confidently, "no matter how much I expected. Besides, I have already heard him speak."

"I don't mean that, I don't mean he is disappointing as a speaker. Stanton is a great orator, I think. Most of those Southerners are, and he's the only real orator I ever heard. But what I mean is, that he does n't go into things impulsively; he first considers himself, and then he considers every other side of the question before he commits himself to it. Before he launches out on a popular wave he tries to find out where it is going to land him. He likes the sort of popular wave that carries him along with it where every one can see him; he doesn't fancy being hurled up on the beach with his mouth full of sand."

"You are saying that he is selfish, self-seeking?" Arkwright demanded with a challenge in his voice. "I thought you were his friend."

"Yes, he is selfish, and yes, I am his friend," the young man answered, smiling; "at least, he seems willing to be mine. I am saying nothing against him that I have not said to him. If you'll come back with me up the elevator I'll tell him he's a self-seeker and selfish, and with no thought above his own interests. He won't mind. He'd say I cannot comprehend his motives. Why, you've only to look at his record. When the Venezuelan message came out he attacked the President and declared he was trying to make political capital and to drag us into war, and that what we wanted was arbitration; but when the President brought out the Arbitration Treaty he attacked that too in the Senate and destroyed it. Why? Not because he had convictions, but because the President had refused a foreign appointment to a friend of his in the South. He has been a free silver man for the last ten years, he comes from a free silver state, and the members of the legislature that elected him were all for silver, but this last election his Wall Street friends got hold of him and worked on his feelings, and he repudiated his party, his state, and his constituents and came out for gold."

"Well, but surely," Arkwright objected, "that took courage? To own that for ten years you had been wrong, and to come out for the right at the last."

Livingstone stared and shrugged his shoulders. "It's all a question of motives," he said indifferently. "I don't want to shatter your idol; I only want to save you from counting too much on him."

When Arkwright called on the morrow Senator Stanton was not at home, and the day following he was busy, and could give him only a brief interview. There were previous engagements and other difficulties in the way of his going which he had not foreseen, he said, and he feared he should have to postpone his visit to Cuba indefinitely. He asked if Mr.

Arkwright would be so kind as to call again within a week; he would then be better able to give him a definite answer.

Arkwright left the apartment with a sensation of such keen disappointment that it turned him ill and dizzy. He felt that the great purpose of his life was being played with and put aside. But he had not selfish resentment on his own account; he was only the more determined to persevere. He considered new arguments and framed new appeals; and one moment blamed himself bitterly for having foolishly discouraged the statesman by too vivid pictures of the horrors he might encounter, and the next, questioned if he had not been too practical and so failed because he had not made the terrible need of immediate help his sole argument. Every hour wasted in delay meant, as he knew, the sacrifice of many lives, and there were other, more sordid and more practical, reasons for speedy action. For his supply of money was running low and there was now barely enough remaining to carry him through the month of travel he had planned to take at Stanton's side. What would happen to him when that

momentous trip was over was of no consequence. He would have done the work as
far as his small share in it lay, he would have
set in motion a great power that was to move
Congress and the people of the United States
to action. If he could but do that, what
became of him counted for nothing.

But at the end of the week his fears and
misgivings were scattered gloriously and a
single line from the senator set his heart
leaping and brought him to his knees in gratitude and thanksgiving. On returning one
afternoon to the mean lodging into which he
had moved to save his money, he found a
telegram from Stanton and he tore it open
trembling between hope and fear.

"Have arranged to leave for Tampa with
you Monday, at midnight" it read. "Call for
me at ten o'clock same evening. — STANTON."

Arkwright read the message three times.
There was a heavy, suffocating pressure at
his heart as though it had ceased beating.
He sank back limply upon the edge of his
bed and clutching the piece of paper in his
two hands spoke the words aloud triumphantly as though to assure himself that they

The Man with One Talent

were true. Then a flood of unspeakable relief, of happiness and gratitude, swept over him, and he turned and slipped to the floor, burying his face in the pillow, and wept out his thanks upon his knees.

A man so deeply immersed in public affairs as was Stanton and with such a multiplicity of personal interests, could not prepare to absent himself for a month without his intention becoming known, and on the day when he was to start for Tampa the morning newspapers proclaimed the fact that he was about to visit Cuba. They gave to his mission all the importance and display that Arkwright had foretold. Some of the newspapers stated that he was going as a special commissioner of the President to study and report; others that he was acting in behalf of the Cuban legation in Washington and had plenipotentiary powers. Opposition organs suggested that he was acting in the interests of the sugar trust, and his own particular organ declared that it was his intention to free Cuba at the risk of his own freedom, safety, and even life.

The Spanish minister in Washington sent

The Man with One Talent

a cable for publication to Madrid, stating that a distinguished American statesman was about to visit Cuba, to investigate, and, later, to deny the truth of the disgraceful libels published concerning the Spanish officials on the island by the papers of the United States. At the same time he cabled in cipher to the captain-general in Havana to see that the distinguished statesman was closely spied upon from the moment of his arrival until his departure, and to place on the "suspect" list all Americans and Cubans who ventured to give him any information.

The afternoon papers enlarged on the importance of the visit and on the good that would surely come of it. They told that Senator Stanton had refused to be interviewed or to disclose the object of his journey. But it was enough, they said, that some one in authority was at last to seek out the truth, and added that no one would be listened to with greater respect than would the Southern senator. On this all the editorial writers were agreed. The day passed drearily for Arkwright. Early in the morning he packed his valise and paid his landlord, and for the remainder of the day walked the streets or sat in the hotel corridor waiting impatiently for each fresh edition of the papers. In them he read the signs of the great upheaval of popular feeling that was to restore peace and health and plenty to the island for which he had given his last three years of energy and life.

He was trembling with excitement, as well as with the cold, when at ten o'clock precisely he stood at Senator Stanton's door. He had forgotten to eat his dinner, and the warmth of the dimly lit hall and the odor of rich food which was wafted from an inner room touched his senses with tantalizing comfort.

"The senator says you are to come this way, sir," the servant directed. He took Arkwright's valise from his hand and parted the heavy curtains that hid the dining-room, and Arkwright stepped in between them and then stopped in some embarrassment. He found himself in the presence of a number of gentlemen seated at a long dinner-table, who turned their heads as he entered and peered at him through the smoke that floated

9   129

in light layers above the white cloth. The dinner had been served, but the senator's guests still sat with their chairs pushed back from a table lighted by candles under yellow shades, and covered with beautiful flowers and with bottles of varied sizes in stands of quaint and intricate design. Senator Stanton's tall figure showed dimly through the smoke, and his deep voice hailed Arkwright cheerily from the farther end of the room. "This way, Mr. Arkwright," he said. "I have a chair waiting for you here." He grasped Arkwright's hand warmly and pulled him into the vacant place at his side. An elderly gentleman on Arkwright's other side moved to make more room for him and shoved a liqueur glass toward him with a friendly nod and pointed at an open box of cigars. He was a fine-looking man, and Arkwright noticed that he was regarding him with a glance of the keenest interest. All of those at the table were men of twice Arkwright's age, except Livingstone, whom he recognized and who nodded to him pleasantly and at the same time gave an order to a servant, pointing at Arkwright as he did so. Some of the gentlemen wore their business suits, and one opposite Arkwright was still in his overcoat, and held his hat in his hand. These latter seemed to have arrived after the dinner had begun, for they formed a second line back of those who had places at the table; they all seemed to know one another and were talking with much vivacity and interest.

Stanton did not attempt to introduce Arkwright to his guests individually, but said: "Gentlemen, this is Mr. Arkwright, of whom I have been telling you, the young gentleman who has done such magnificent work for the cause of Cuba." Those who caught Arkwright's eye nodded to him, and others raised their glasses at him, but with a smile that he could not understand. It was as though they all knew something concerning him of which he was ignorant. He noted that the faces of some were strangely familiar, and he decided that he must have seen their portraits in the public prints. After he had introduced Arkwright, the senator drew his chair slightly away from him and turned in what seemed embarrassment to the man on his other side. The elderly gentleman next to Arkwright filled his glass, a servant placed a small cup of coffee at his elbow, and he lit a cigar and looked about him.

"You must find this weather very trying after the tropics," his neighbor said.

Arkwright assented cordially. The brandy was flowing through his veins and warming him; he forgot that he was hungry, and the kind, interested glances of those about him set him at his ease. It was a propitious start, he thought, a pleasant leave-taking for the senator and himself, full of good will and good wishes.

He turned toward Stanton and waited until he had ceased speaking.

"The papers have begun well, have n't they?" he asked, eagerly.

He had spoken in a low voice, almost in a whisper, but those about the table seemed to have heard him, for there was silence instantly and when he glanced up he saw the eyes of all turned upon him and he noticed on their faces the same smile he had seen there when he entered.

"Yes," Stanton answered constrainedly.

The Man with One Talent

"Yes, I —" he lowered his voice, but the silence still continued. Stanton had his eyes fixed on the table, but now he frowned and half rose from his chair.

"I want to speak with you, Arkwright," he said. "Suppose we go into the next room. I'll be back in a moment," he added, nodding to the others.

But the man on his right removed his cigar from his lips and said in an undertone, "No, sit down, stay where you are;" and the elderly gentleman at Arkwright's side laid his hand detainingly on his arm. "Oh, you won't take Mr. Arkwright away from us, Stanton?" he asked, smiling.

Stanton shrugged his shoulders and sat down again, and there was a moment's pause. It was broken by the man in the overcoat, who laughed.

"He's paying you a compliment, Mr. Arkwright," he said. He pointed with his cigar to the gentleman at Arkwright's side.

"I don't understand," Arkwright answered doubtfully.

"It's a compliment to your eloquence — he's afraid to leave you alone with the senator. Livingstone's been telling us that you are a better talker than Stanton." Arkwright turned a troubled countenance toward the men about the table, and then toward Livingstone, but that young man had his eyes fixed gravely on the glasses before him and did not raise them.

Arkwright felt a sudden, unreasonable fear of the circle of strong-featured, serene and confident men about him. They seemed to be making him the subject of a jest, to be enjoying something among themselves of which he was in ignorance, but which concerned him closely. He turned a white face toward Stanton.

"You don't mean," he began piteously, "that — that you are not going? Is that it — tell me — is that what you wanted to say?"

Stanton shifted in his chair and muttered some words between his lips, then turned toward Arkwright and spoke quite clearly and distinctly.

"I am very sorry, Mr. Arkwright," he said, "but I am afraid I'll have to disappoint you. Reasons I cannot now explain have arisen which make my going impossible —

quite impossible," he added firmly — "not only now, but later," he went on quickly, as Arkwright was about to interrupt him.

Arkwright made no second attempt to speak. He felt the muscles of his face working and the tears coming to his eyes, and to hide his weakness he twisted in his chair and sat staring ahead of him with his back turned to the table. He heard Livingstone's voice break the silence with some hurried question, and immediately his embarrassment was hidden in a murmur of answers and the moving of glasses as the men shifted in their chairs and the laughter and talk went on as briskly as before. Arkwright saw a sideboard before him and a servant arranging some silver on one of the shelves. He watched the man do this with a concentrated interest as though the dull, numbed feeling in his brain caught at the trifle in order to put off, as long as possible, the consideration of the truth.

And then beyond the sideboard and the tapestry on the wall above it, he saw the sun shining down upon the island of Cuba, he saw the royal palms waving and bending, the dusty columns of Spanish infantry crawling along the white roads and leaving blazing huts and smoking cane-fields in their wake; he saw skeletons of men and women seeking for food among the refuse of the street; he heard the order given to the firing squad, the splash of the bullets as they scattered the plaster on the prison wall, and he saw a kneeling figure pitch forward on its face, with a useless bandage tied across its sightless eyes.

Senator Stanton brought him back with a sharp shake of the shoulder. He had also turned his back on the others, and was leaning forward with his elbows on his knees. He spoke rapidly, and in a voice only slightly raised above a whisper.

"I am more than sorry, Arkwright," he said earnestly. "You must n't blame me altogether. I have had a hard time of it this afternoon. I wanted to go. I really wanted to go. The thing appealed to me, it touched me, it seemed as if I owed it to myself to do it. But they were too many for me," he added with a backward toss of his head toward the men around his table.

"If the papers had not told on me I could have got well away," he went on in an eager tone, "but as soon as they read of it, they came here straight from their offices. You know who they are, don't you?" he asked, and even in his earnestness there was an added touch of importance in his tone as he spoke the name of his party's leader, of men who stood prominently in Wall Street and who were at the head of great trusts.

"You see how it is," he said with a shrug of his shoulders. "They have enormous interests at stake. They said I would drag them into war, that I would disturb values, that the business interests of the country would suffer. I'm under obligations to most of them, they have advised me in financial matters, and they threatened — they threatened to make it unpleasant for me." His voice hardened and he drew in his breath quickly, and laughed. "You would n't understand if I were to tell you. It's rather involved. And after all, they may be right, agitation may be bad for the country. And your party leader after all is your party leader, is n't he, and if he says 'no' what are you to do? My sympathies are just as keen for these poor women and children as ever, but as these men say, 'charity begins at home,' and we must n't do anything to bring on war prices again, or to send stocks tumbling about our heads, must we?" He leaned back in his chair again and sighed. "Sympathy is an expensive luxury, I find," he added.

Arkwright rose stiffly and pushed Stanton away from him with his hand. He moved like a man coming out of a dream.

"Don't talk to me like that," he said in a low voice. The noise about the table ended on the instant, but Arkwright did not notice that it had ceased. "You know I don't understand that," he went on; "what does it matter to me?" He put his hand up to the side of his face and held it there, looking down at Stanton. He had the dull, heavy look in his eyes of a man who has just come through an operation under some heavy drug. "'Wall Street,' 'trusts,' 'party leaders,'" he repeated, "what are they to me? The words don't reach me, they have lost their meaning, it is a language I have forgotten, thank God!" he added. He turned and moved his eyes around the table, scanning the faces of the men before him.

"Yes, you are twelve to one," he said at last, still speaking dully and in a low voice, as though he were talking to himself. "You have won a noble victory, gentlemen. I congratulate you. But I do not blame you, we are all selfish and self-seeking. I thought I was working only for Cuba, but I was working for myself, just as you are. I wanted to feel that it was I who had helped to bring relief to that plague-spot, that it was through my efforts the help had come. Yes, if he had done as I asked, I suppose I would have taken the credit."

He swayed slightly, and to steady himself caught at the back of his chair. But at the same moment his eyes glowed fiercely and he held himself erect again. He pointed with his finger at the circle of great men who sat looking up at him in curious silence.

"You are like a ring of gamblers around a gaming table," he cried wildly, "who see nothing but the green cloth and the wheel and the piles of money before them, who forget in watching the money rise and fall, that outside the sun is shining, that human beings are sick and suffering, that men are giving their lives for an idea, for a sentiment, for a flag. You are the money-changers in the temple of this great republic and the day will come, I pray to God, when you will be scourged and driven out with whips. Do you think you can form combines and deals that will cheat you into heaven? Can your 'trusts' save your souls — is 'Wall Street' the strait and narrow road to salvation?"

The men about the table leaned back and stared at Arkwright in as great amazement as though he had violently attempted an assault upon their pockets, or had suddenly gone mad in their presence. Some of them frowned, and others appeared not to have heard, and others smiled grimly and waited for him to continue as though they were spectators at a play.

The political leader broke the silence with a low aside to Stanton. "Does the gentleman belong to the Salvation Army?" he asked.

Arkwright whirled about and turned upon him fiercely.

You are like a ring of gamblers around a gaming table.

The Man with One Talent

"Old gods give way to new gods," he cried. "Here is your brother. I am speaking for him. Do you ever think of him? How dare you sneer at me?" he cried. "You can crack your whip over that man's head and turn him from what in his heart and conscience he knows is right; you can crack your whip over the men who call themselves free-born American citizens and who have made you their boss — sneer at them if you like, but you have no collar on my neck. If you are a leader, why don't you lead your people to what is good and noble? Why do you stop this man in the work God sent him here to do? You would make a party hack of him, a political prostitute, something lower than the woman who walks the streets. She sells her body — this man is selling his soul."

He turned, trembling and quivering, and shook his finger above the upturned face of the senator.

"What have you done with your talents, Stanton?" he cried. "What have you done with your talents?"

The man in the overcoat struck the table

before him with his fist so that the glasses rang.

"By God," he laughed, "I call him a better speaker than Stanton! Livingstone's right, he *is* better than Stanton — but he lacks Stanton's knack of making himself popular," he added. He looked around the table inviting approbation with a smile, but no one noticed him, nor spoke to break the silence.

Arkwright heard the words dully and felt that he was being mocked. He covered his face with his hands and stood breathing brokenly; his body was still trembling with an excitement he could not master.

Stanton rose from his chair and shook him by the shoulder. "Are you mad, Arkwright?" he cried. "You have no right to insult my guests or me. Be calm — control yourself."

"What does it matter what I say?" Arkwright went on desperately. "I am mad. Yes, that is it, I am mad. They have won and I have lost, and it drove me beside myself. I counted on you. I knew that no one else could let my people go. But I'll not trouble you again. I wish you good-night, sir, and good-bye. If I have been unjust, you must forget it."

He turned sharply, but Stanton placed a detaining hand on his shoulder. "Wait," he commanded querulously; "where are you going? Will you, still —?"

Arkwright bowed his head. "Yes," he answered. "I have but just time now to catch our train — my train, I mean."

He looked up at Stanton and taking his hand in both of his, drew the man toward him. All the wildness and intolerance in his manner had passed, and as he raised his eyes they were full of a firm resolve.

"Come," he said simply; "there is yet time. Leave these people behind you. What can you answer when they ask what have you done with your talents?"

"Good God, Arkwright," the senator exclaimed angrily, pulling his hand away; "don't talk like a hymn-book, and don't make another scene. What you ask is impossible. Tell me what I can do to help you in any other way, and —"

"Come," repeated the young man firmly.

143

"The world may judge you by what you do to-night."

Stanton looked at the boy for a brief moment with a strained and eager scrutiny, and then turned away abruptly and shook his head in silence, and Arkwright passed around the table and on out of the room.

A month later, as the Southern senator was passing through the reading-room of the Union Club, Livingstone beckoned to him, and handing him an afternoon paper pointed at a paragraph in silence. The paragraph was dated Sagua la Grande, and read:

"The body of Henry Arkwright, an American civil engineer, was brought into Sagua to-day by a Spanish column. It was found lying in a road three miles beyond the line of forts. Arkwright was surprised by a guerilla force while attempting to make his way to the insurgent camp, and on resisting was shot. The body has been handed over to the American consul for interment. It is badly mutilated."

Stanton lowered the paper and stood staring out of the window at the falling snow and

The Man with One Talent

the cheery lights and bustling energy of the avenue.

"Poor fellow," he said, "he wanted so much to help them. And he did n't accomplish anything, did he?"

Livingstone stared at the older man and laughed shortly.

"Well, I don't know," he said. "He died. Some of us only live."

The Vagrant

HIS Excellency Sir Charles Greville,
K. C. M. G., Governor of the Windless
Islands, stood upon the veranda of Government House surveying the new day with
critical and searching eyes. Sir Charles had
been so long absolute monarch of the Windless Isles that he had assumed unconsciously
a mental attitude of suzerainty over even the
glittering waters of the Caribbean Sea, and
the coral reefs under the waters, and the rain-
bow skies that floated above them. But on
this particular morning not even the critical
eye of the Governor could distinguish a single
flaw in the tropical landscape before him.

The lawn at his feet ran down to meet the
dazzling waters of the bay, the blue waters of
the bay ran to meet a great stretch of absinthe
green, the green joined a fairy sky of pink

and gold and saffron.   Islands of coral floated
on the sea of absinthe, and derelict clouds of
mother-of-pearl swung low above them, start-
ing from nowhere and going nowhere, but
drifting beautifully, like giant soap-bubbles
of light and color.   Where the lawn touched
the waters of the bay the cocoanut-palms
reached their crooked lengths far up into the
sunshine, and as the sea-breeze stirred their
fronds they filled the hot air with whispers
and murmurs like the fluttering of many fans.
Nature smiled boldly upon the Governor,
confident in her bountiful beauty, as though
she said, " Surely you cannot but be pleased
with me to-day."   And, as though in answer,
the critical and searching glance of Sir
Charles relaxed.

The crunching of the gravel and the rattle
of the sentry's musket at salute recalled him
to his high office and to the duties of the
morning.   He waved his hand, and, as though
it were a wand, the sentry moved again,
making his way to the kitchen-garden, and
so around Government House and back to
the lawn-tennis court, maintaining in his soli-
tary pilgrimage the dignity of her Majesty's

representative, as well as her Majesty's power over the Windless Isles.

The Governor smiled slightly, with the ease of mind of one who finds all things good. Supreme authority, surroundings of endless beauty, the respectful, even humble, deference of his inferiors, and never even an occasional visit from a superior, had in four years lowered him into a bed of ease and self-satisfaction. He was cut off from the world, and yet of it. Each month there came, *via* Jamaica, the three weeks' old copy of *The Weekly Times;* he subscribed to Mudie's Colonial Library; and from the States he had imported an American lawn-mower, the mechanism of which no one as yet understood. Within his own borders he had created a healthy, orderly seaport out of what had been a sink of fever and a refuge for all the ne'er-do-wells and fugitive revolutionists of Central America.

He knew, as he sat each evening on his veranda, looking across the bay, that in the world beyond the pink and gold sunset men were still panting, struggling, and starving; crises were rising and passing; strikes and

148

panics, wars and the rumors of wars, swept
from continent to continent; a plague crept
through India; a filibuster with five hundred
men at his back crossed an imaginary line
and stirred the world from Cape Town to
London; Emperors were crowned; the good
Queen celebrated the longest reign; and a
captain of artillery imprisoned in a swampy
island in the South Atlantic caused two
hemispheres to clamor for his rescue, and lit
a race war that stretched from Algiers to the
boulevards.

And yet, at the Windless Isles, all these
happenings seemed to Sir Charles like the
morning's memory of a dream. For these
things never crossed the ring of the coral
reefs; he saw them only as pictures in an
illustrated paper a month old. And he was
pleased to find that this was so. He was
sufficient to himself, with his own responsi-
bilities and social duties and public works.
He was a man in authority, who said to
others, "Come!" and "Go!" Under him
were commissioners, and under the commissioners district inspectors and boards of edu-
cation and of highways. For the better

health of the colony he had planted trees
that sucked the malaria from the air; for its
better morals he had substituted as a Sunday
amusement cricket-matches for cock-fights;
and to keep it at peace he had created a local
constabulary of native negroes, and had
dressed them in the cast-off uniforms of London policemen. His handiwork was everywhere, and his interest was all sunk in his
handiwork. The days passed gorgeous with
sunshine, the nights breathed with beauty.
It was an existence of leisurely occupation,
and one that promised no change, and he
was content.

As it was Thursday, the Council met that
morning, and some questions of moment to
the colony were to be brought up for consideration. The question of the dog-tax was
one which perplexed Sir Charles most particularly. The two Councillors elected by the
people and the three appointed by the crown
had disagreed as to this tax. Of the five
hundred British subjects at the seaport, all
but ten were owners of dogs, and it had
occurred to Sassoon, the chemist, that a tax
of half-a-crown a year on each of these dogs

would meet the expense of extending the
oyster-shell road to the new cricket-grounds.
To this Snellgrove, who held the contract for
the narrow-gauge railroad, agreed; but the
three crown Councillors opposed the tax
vigorously, on the ground that as scavengers
alone the dogs were a boon to the colony
and should be encouraged. The fact that
each of these gentlemen owned not only one,
but several dogs of high pedigree made their
position one of great delicacy.

There was no way by which the Governor
could test the popular will in the matter, except through his secretary, Mr. Clarges, who,
at the cricket-match between the local eleven
and the officers and crew of H. M. S. *Partridge*, had been informed by the other
owners of several fox-terriers that, in their
opinion, the tax was a piece of " condemned
tommy-rot." From this the Governor judged
that it would not prove a popular measure.
As he paced the veranda, drawing deliberately
on his cigar, and considering to which party
he should give the weight of his final support,
his thoughts were disturbed by the approach
of a stranger, who advanced along the gravel

The Vagrant

walk, guarded on either side by one of the
local constabulary. The stranger was young
and of poor appearance. His bare feet were
bound in a pair of the rope sandals worn by
the natives, his clothing was of torn and soiled
drill, and he fanned his face nonchalantly
with a sombrero of battered and shapeless
felt.

Sir Charles halted in his walk, and holding
his cigar behind his back, addressed himself
to the sergeant.

"A vagrant?" he asked.

The words seemed to bear some amusing
significance to the stranger, for his face lit
instantly with a sweet and charming smile,
and while he turned to hear the sergeant's
reply, he regarded him with a kindly and
affectionate interest.

"Yes, your Excellency."

The Governor turned to the prisoner.

"Do you know the law of this colony
regarding vagrants?"

"I do not," the young man answered. His
tone was politely curious, and suggested that
he would like to be further informed as to
the local peculiarities of a foreign country.

152

The Vagrant

"After two weeks' residence," the Governor recited, impressively, "all able-bodied persons who will not work are put to work or deported. Have you made any effort to find work?"

Again the young man smiled charmingly. He shook his head and laughed. "Oh dear no," he said.

The laugh struck the Governor as impertinent.

"Then you must leave by the next mail-steamer, if you have any money to pay your passage, or, if you have no money, you must go to work on the roads. Have you any money?"

"If I had, I would n't — be a vagrant," the young man answered. His voice was low and singularly sweet. It seemed to suit the indolence of his attitude and the lazy, inconsequent smile. "I called on our consular agent here," he continued, leisurely, "to write a letter home for money, but he was disgracefully drunk, so I used his official note-paper to write to the State Department about him, instead."

The Governor's deepest interest was aroused.

The Vagrant

The American consular agent was one of the severest trials he was forced to endure.

"You are not a British subject, then? Ah, I see — and — er — your representative was unable to assist you?"

"He was drunk," the young man repeated, placidly. "He has been drunk ever since I have been here, particularly in the mornings." He halted, as though the subject had lost interest for him, and gazed pleasantly at the sunny bay and up at the moving palms.

"Then," said the Governor, as though he had not been interrupted, "as you have no means of support, you will help support the colony until you can earn money to leave it. That will do, sergeant."

The young man placed his hat upon his head and turned to move away, but at the first step he swayed suddenly and caught at the negro's shoulder, clasping his other hand across his eyes. The sergeant held him by the waist, and looked up at the Governor with some embarrassment.

"The young gentleman has not been well, Sir Charles," he said, apologetically.

The stranger straightened himself up and

smiled vaguely. "I'm all right," he murmured. "Sun's too hot."

"Sit down," said the Governor.

He observed the stranger more closely. He noticed now that beneath the tan his face was delicate and finely cut, and that his yellow hair clung closely to a well-formed head.

"He seems faint. Has he had anything to eat?" asked the Governor.

The sergeant grinned guiltily. "Yes, Sir Charles; we've been feeding him at the barracks. It's fever, sir."

Sir Charles was not unacquainted with fallen gentlemen, "beach-combers," "remittance men," and vagrants who had known better days, and there had been something winning in this vagrant's smile, and, moreover, he had reported that thorn in his flesh, the consular agent, to the proper authorities.

He conceived an interest in a young man who, though with naked feet, did not hesitate to correspond with his Minister of Foreign Affairs.

"How long have you been ill?" he asked.

The young man looked up from where he had sunk on the steps, and roused himself with a shrug. "It does n't matter," he said. "I've had a touch of Chagres ever since I was on the Isthmus. I was at work there on the railroad."

"Did you come here from Colon?"

"No; I worked up the Pacific side. I was clerking with Rossner Brothers at Amapala for a while, because I speak a little German, and then I footed it over to Puerto Cortez and got a job with the lottery people. They gave me twenty dollars a month gold for rolling the tickets, and I put it all in the drawing, and won as much as ten." He laughed, and sitting erect, drew from his pocket a roll of thin green papers. "These are for the next drawing," he said. "Have some?" he added. He held them towards the negro sergeant, who, under the eye of the Governor, resisted, and then spread the tickets on his knee like a hand at cards. "I stand to win a lot with these," he said, with a cheerful sigh. "You see, until the list's published I'm prospectively worth twenty thousand dollars. And," he added, "I break stones in the sun." He rose unsteadily, and saluted the Governor with a

156

nod. "Good-morning, sir," he said, "and
thank you."

"Wait," Sir Charles commanded. A new
form of punishment had suggested itself, in
which justice was tempered with mercy.
"Can you work one of your American lawn-
mowers?" he asked.

The young man laughed delightedly. "I
never tried," he said, "but I've seen it done."

"If you've been ill, it would be murder
to put you on the shell road." The Governor's dignity relaxed into a smile. "I don't
desire international complications," he said.
"Sergeant, take this — him — to the kitchen,
and tell Corporal Mallon to give him that
American lawn-mowing machine. Possibly
he may understand its mechanism. Mallon
only cuts holes in the turf with it." And he
waved his hand in dismissal, and as the three
men moved away he buried himself again in
the perplexities of the dog-tax.

Ten minutes later the deliberations of the
Council were disturbed by a loud and per-
sistent rattle, like the whir of a Maxim gun,
which proved, on investigation, to arise from
the American lawn-mower. The vagrant was

propelling it triumphantly across the lawn, and gazing down at it with the same fond pride with which a nursemaid leans over the perambulator to observe her lusty and gurgling charge.

The Councillors had departed, Sir Charles was thinking of breakfast, the Maxim-like lawn-mower still irritated the silent hush of midday, when from the waters of the inner harbor there came suddenly the sharp report of a saluting gun and the rush of falling anchor-chains. There was still a week to pass before the mail-steamer should arrive, and H. M. S. *Partridge* had departed for Nassau. Besides these ships, no other vessel had skirted the buoys of the bay in eight long smiling months. Mr. Clarges, the secretary, with an effort to appear calm, and the orderly, suffocated with the news, entered through separate doors at the same instant.

The secretary filed his report first. "A yacht's just anchored in the bay, Sir Charles," he said.

The orderly's face fell. He looked aggrieved. "An American yacht," he corrected.

The Vagrant

"And much larger than the *Partridge*," continued the secretary.

The orderly took a hasty glance back over his shoulder. "She has her launch lowered already, sir," he said.

Outside the whir of the lawn-mower continued undisturbed. Sir Charles reached for his marine-glass, and the three men hurried to the veranda.

"It looks like a man-of-war," said Sir Charles. "No," he added, adjusting the binocular; "she's a yacht. She flies the New York Yacht Club pennant — now she's showing the owner's absent pennant. He must have left in the launch. He's coming ashore now."

"He seems in a bit of a hurry," growled Mr. Clarges.

"Those Americans always — " murmured Sir Charles from behind the binocular. He did not quite know that he enjoyed this sudden onslaught upon the privacy of his harbor and port.

It was in itself annoying, and he was further annoyed to find that it could in the least degree disturb his poise.

The Vagrant

The launch was growing instantly larger, like an express train approaching a station at full speed; her flags flew out as flat as pieces of painted tin; her bits of brass-work flashed like fire. Already the ends of the wharves were white with groups of natives.

"You might think he was going to ram the town," suggested the secretary.

"Oh, I say," he exclaimed, in remonstrance, "he's making in for your private wharf."

The Governor was rearranging the focus of the glass with nervous fingers. "I believe," he said, "no — yes — upon my word, there are — there are ladies in that launch!"

"Ladies, sir!" The secretary threw a hasty glance at the binocular, but it was in immediate use.

The clatter of the lawn-mower ceased suddenly, and the relief of its silence caused the Governor to lower his eyes. He saw the lawn-mower lying prostrate on the grass. The vagrant had vanished.

There was a sharp tinkle of bells, and the launch slipped up to the wharf and halted as softly as a bicycle. A man in a yachting-suit jumped from her, and making some

The Vagrant

laughing speech to the two women in the stern, walked briskly across the lawn, taking a letter from his pocket as he came. Sir Charles awaited him gravely; the occupants of the launch had seen him, and it was too late to retreat.

" Sir Charles Greville, I believe," said the yachtsman. He bowed, and ran lightly up the steps. " I am Mr. Robert Collier, from New York," he said. " I have a letter to you from your ambassador at Washington. If you 'll pardon me, I 'll present it in person. I had meant to leave it, but seeing you —" He paused, and gave the letter in his hand to Sir Charles, who waved him towards his library.

Sir Charles scowled at the letter through his monocle, and then shook hands with his visitor. " I am very glad to see you, Mr. Collier," he said. " He says here you are preparing a book on our colonies in the West Indies." He tapped the letter with his monocle. " I am sure I shall be most happy to assist you with any information in my power."

" Well, I am writing a book — yes," Mr.

Collier observed, doubtfully, " but it's a log-book. This trip I am on pleasure bent, and I also wish to consult with you on a personal matter. However, that can wait." He glanced out of the windows to where the launch lay in the sun. " My wife came ashore with me, Sir Charles," he said, " so that in case there was a Lady Greville, Mrs. Collier could call on her, and we could ask if you would waive etiquette and do us the honor to dine with us to-night on the yacht — that is, if you are not engaged."

Sir Charles smiled. " There is no Lady Greville," he said, " and I personally do not think I am engaged elsewhere." He paused in thought, as though to make quite sure he was not. "No," he added, " I have no other engagement. I will come with pleasure."

Sir Charles rose and clapped his hands for the orderly. " Possibly the ladies will come up to the veranda?" he asked. " I cannot allow them to remain at the end of my wharf." He turned, and gave directions to the orderly to bring limes and bottles of soda and ice, and led the way across the lawn.

The Vagrant

Mrs. Collier and her friend had not explored the grounds of Government House for over ten minutes before Sir Charles felt that many years ago he had personally arranged their visit, that he had known them for even a longer time, and that, now that they had finally arrived, they must never depart.

To them there was apparently nothing on his domain which did not thrill with delightful interest. They were as eager as two children at a pantomime, and as unconscious. As a rule, Sir Charles had found it rather difficult to meet the women of his colony on a path which they were capable of treading intelligently. In fairness to them, he had always sought out some topic in which they could take an equal part — something connected with the conduct of children, or the better ventilation of the new school-house and chapel. But these new-comers did not require him to select topics of conversation; they did not even wait for him to finish those which he himself introduced. They flitted from one end of the garden to the other with the eagerness of two midshipmen on shore leave, and they found something to enjoy in what seemed to the Governor the most commonplace of things. The Zouave uniform of the sentry, the old Spanish cannon converted into peaceful gate-posts, the aviary with its screaming paroquets, the botanical station, and even the ice-machine were all objects of delight.

On the other hand, the interior of the famous palace, which had been sent out complete from London, and which was wont to fill the wives of the colonials with awe or to reduce them to whispers, for some reason failed of its effect. But they said they "loved" the large gold V. R.'s on the back of the Councillors' chairs, and they exclaimed aloud over the red leather despatch-boxes and the great seal of the colony, and the mysterious envelopes marked "On her Majesty's service."

"Isn't it too exciting, Florence?" demanded Mrs. Collier. "This is the table where Sir Charles sits and writes letters ' on her Majesty's service,' and presses these buttons, and war-ships spring up in perfect shoals. Oh, Robert," she sighed, "I do wish you had been a Governor!"

The Vagrant

The young lady called Florence stood looking down into the great arm-chair in front of the Governor's table.

"May I?" she asked. She slid fearlessly in between the oak arms of the chair and smiled about her. Afterwards Sir Charles remembered her as she appeared at that moment with the red leather of the chair behind her, with her gloved hands resting on the carved oak, and her head on one side, smiling up at him. She gazed with large eyes at the blue linen envelopes, the stiff documents in red tape, the tray of black sand, and the goose-quill pens.

"I am now the Countess Zika," she announced; "no, I am Diana of the Crossways, and I mean to discover a state secret and sell it to the *Daily Telegraph*. Sir Charles," she demanded, "if I press this electric button is war declared anywhere, or what happens?"

"That second button," said Sir Charles, after deliberate scrutiny, "is the one which communicates with the pantry."

The Governor would not consider their returning to the yacht for luncheon.

The Vagrant

"You might decide to steam away as suddenly as you came," he said, gallantly, "and I cannot take that chance. This is Bachelor's Hall, so you must pardon my people if things do not go very smoothly." He himself led them to the great guest-chamber, where there had not been a guest for many years, and he noticed, as though for the first time, that the halls through which they passed were bare, and that the floor was littered with unpacked boxes and gun-cases. He also observed for the first time that maps of the colony, with the coffee-plantations and mahogany belt marked in different inks, were not perhaps so decorative as pictures and mirrors and family portraits. And he could have wished that the native servants had not stared so admiringly at the guests, nor directed each other in such aggressive whispers. On those other occasions, when the wives of the Councillors came to the semi-annual dinners, the native servants had seemed adequate to all that was required of them. He recollected with a flush that in the town these semi-annual dinners were described as banquets. He

wondered if to these visitors from the outside world it was all equally provincial.

But their enjoyment was apparently un-
feigned and generous. It was evident that
they had known each other for many years,
yet they received every remark that any of
them made as though it had been pronounced
by a new and interesting acquaintance. Sir
Charles found it rather difficult to keep up
with the talk across the table, they changed
the subject so rapidly, and they half spoke
of so many things without waiting to explain.
He could not at once grasp the fact that
people who had no other position in the
world save that of observers were speaking
so authoritatively of public men and public
measures. He found, to his delight, that for
the first time in several years he was not pre-
siding at his own table, and that his guests
seemed to feel no awe of him.

"What's the use of a yacht nowadays?"
Collier was saying — "what's the use of a
yacht, when you can go to sleep in a wagon-
lit at the Gare du Nord, and wake up at
Vladivostok? And look at the time it saves;
eleven days to Gib, six to Port Said, and

fifteen to Colombo — there you are, only half-way around, and you 're already sixteen days behind the man in the wagon-lit."

" But nobody wants to go to Vladivostok," said Miss Cameron, " or anywhere else in a wagon-lit. But with a yacht you can explore out-of-the-way places, and you meet new and interesting people. We would n't have met Sir Charles if we had waited for a wagon-lit." She bowed her head to the Governor, and he smiled with gratitude. He had lost Mr. Collier somewhere in the Indian Ocean, and he was glad she had brought them back to the Windless Isles once more.

" And again I repeat that the answer to that is, ' Why not? said the March Hare,' " remarked Mr. Collier, determinedly.

The answer, as an answer, did not strike Sir Charles as a very good one. But the ladies seemed to comprehend, for Miss Cameron said : " Did I tell you about meeting him at Oxford just a few months before his death — at a children's tea-party? He was so sweet and understanding with them ! Two women tried to lionize him, and he ran away and played with the

168

children. I was more glad to meet him than any one I can think of. Not as a personage, you know, but because I felt grateful to him."

"Yes, that way, distinctly," said Mrs. Collier. "I should have felt that way towards Mrs. Ewing more than any one else."

"I know, 'Jackanapes,'" remarked Collier, shortly; "a brutal assault upon the feelings, I say."

"Some one else said it before you, Robert," Mrs. Collier commented, calmly. "Perhaps Sir Charles met him at Apia." They all turned and looked at him. He wished he could say he had met him at Apia. He did not quite see how they had made their way from a children's tea party at Oxford to the South Pacific islands, but he was anxious to join in somewhere with a clever observation. But they never seemed to settle in one place sufficiently long for him to recollect what he knew of it. He hoped they would get around to the west coast of Africa in time. He had been Governor of Sierra Leone for five years.

The Vagrant

His success that night at dinner on the yacht was far better. The others seemed a little tired after the hours of sight-seeing to which he had treated them, and they were content to listen. In the absence of Mr. Clarges, who knew them word by word, he felt free to tell his three stories of life at Sierra Leone. He took his time in the telling, and could congratulate himself that his efforts had never been more keenly appreciated. He felt that he was holding his own.

The night was still and warm, and while the men lingered below at the table, the two women mounted to the deck and watched the lights of the town as they vanished one by one and left the moon in unchallenged possession of the harbor. For a long time Miss Cameron stood silent, looking out across the bay at the shore and the hills beyond. A fish splashed near them, and the sound of oars rose from the mist that floated above the water, until they were muffled in the distance. The palms along the shore glistened like silver, and overhead the Southern Cross shone white against a sky of purple. The silence deepened and continued for so long a time that Mrs. Collier felt its significance, and waited for the girl to end it.

Miss Cameron raised her eyes to the stars and frowned. "I am not surprised that he is content to stay here," she said. "Are you? It is so beautiful, so wonderfully beautiful."

For a moment Mrs. Collier made no answer. "Two years is a long time, Florence," she said; "and he is all I have; he is not only my only brother, he is the only living soul who is related to me. That makes it harder."

The girl seemed to find some implied reproach in the speech, for she turned and looked at her friend closely. "Do you feel it is my fault, Alice?" she asked.

The older woman shook her head. "How could it be your fault?" she answered. "If you couldn't love him enough to marry him, you couldn't, that's all. But that is no reason why he should have hidden himself from all of us. Even if he could not stand being near you, caring as he did, he need

not have treated me so. We have done all
we can do, and Robert has been more than
fine about it. He and his agents have written
to every consul and business house in Central
America, and I don't believe there is a city
that he has n't visited. He has sent him
money and letters to every bank and to every
post-office — "

The girl raised her head quickly.

" — but he never calls for either," Mrs.
Collier continued, " for I know that if he had
read my letters he would have come home."

The girl lifted her head as though she
were about to speak, and then turned and
walked slowly away. After a few moments
she returned, and stood, with her hands
resting on the rail, looking down into the
water. "I wrote him two letters," she said.
In the silence of the night her voice was
unusually clear and distinct. "I — you
make me wonder — if they ever reached
him."

Mrs. Collier, with her eyes fixed upon the
girl, rose slowly from her chair and came
towards her. She reached out her hand
and touched Miss Cameron on the arm.

"Florence," she said, in a whisper, "have you —"

The girl raised her head slowly, and lowered it again. "Yes," she answered; "I told him to come back — to come back to me. Alice," she cried, "I — I begged him to come back!" She tossed her hands apart and again walked rapidly away, leaving the older woman standing motionless.

A moment later, when Sir Charles and Mr. Collier stepped out upon the deck, they discovered the two women standing close together, two white, ghostly figures in the moonlight, and as they advanced towards them they saw Mrs. Collier take the girl for an instant in her arms.

Sir Charles was asking Miss Cameron how long she thought an immigrant should be made to work for his freehold allotment, when Mr. Collier and his wife rose at the same moment and departed on separate errands. They met most mysteriously in the shadow of the wheel-house.

"What is it? Is anything wrong with Florence?" Collier asked, anxiously. "Not homesick, is she?"

The Vagrant

Mrs. Collier put her hands on her husband's shoulders and shook her head.

"Wrong? No, thank Heaven! it's as right as right can be!" she cried. "She's written to him to come back, but he's never answered, and so — and now it's all right."

Mr. Collier gazed blankly at his wife's upturned face. "Well, I don't see that," he remonstrated. "What's the use of her being in love with him now when he can't be found? What? Why did n't she love him two years ago when he was where you could get at him — at her house, for instance. He was there most of his time. She would have saved a lot of trouble. However," he added, energetically, "this makes it absolutely necessary to find that young man and bring him to his senses. We'll search this place for the next few days, and then we'll try the mainland again. I think I'll offer a reward for him, and have it printed in Spanish, and paste it up in all the plazas. We might add a line in English, 'She has changed her mind.' That would bring him home, would n't it?"

The Vagrant

"Don't be unfeeling, Robert," said Mrs. Collier.

Her husband raised his eyes appealingly, and addressed himself to the moon. "I ask you now," he complained, "is that fair to a man who has spent six months on muleback trying to round up a prodigal brother-in-law?"

That same evening, after the ladies had gone below, Mr. Collier asked Sir Charles to assist him in his search for his wife's brother, and Sir Charles heartily promised his most active co-operation. There were several Americans at work in the interior, he said, as overseers on the coffee-plantations. It was possible that the runaway might be among them. It was only that morning, Sir Charles remembered, that an American had been at work "repairing his lawn-mower," as he considerately expressed it. He would send for him on the morrow.

But on the morrow the slave of the lawn-mower was reported on the list of prisoners as "missing," and Corporal Mallon was grieved, but refused to consider himself responsible. Sir Charles himself had allowed the vagrant unusual freedom, and the vagrant had taken advantage of it, and probably escaped to the hills, or up the river to the logwood camp.

"Telegraph a description of him to Inspector Garrett," Sir Charles directed, "and to the heads of all up stations. And when he returns, bring him to me."

So great was his zeal that Sir Charles further offered to join Mr. Collier in his search among the outlying plantations; but Mr. Collier preferred to work alone. He accordingly set out at once, armed with letters to the different district inspectors, and in his absence delegated to Sir Charles the pleasant duty of caring for the wants of Miss Cameron and his wife. Sir Charles regarded the latter as deserving of all sympathy, for Mr. Collier, in his efforts to conceal the fact from the Governor that Florence Cameron was responsible, or in any way concerned, in the disappearance of the missing man, had been too mysterious. Sir Charles was convinced that the fugitive had swindled his brother-in-law and stolen his sister's jewels.

The days which followed were to the Governor days and nights of strange discoveries.

He recognized that the missionaries from the great outside world had invaded his shores and disturbed his gods and temples. Their religion of progress and activity filled him with doubt and unrest.

"In this century," Mr. Collier had declared, "nothing can stand still. It's the same with a corporation, or a country, or a man. We must either march ahead or fall out. We can't mark time. What?"

"Exactly —certainly not," Sir Charles had answered. But in his heart he knew that he himself had been marking time under these soft tropical skies while the world was pushing forward. The thought had not disturbed him before. Now he felt guilty. He conceived a sudden intolerance, if not contempt, for the little village of whitewashed houses, for the rafts of mahogany and of logwood that bumped against the pier-heads, for the sacks of coffee piled high like barricades under the corrugated zinc sheds along the wharf. Each season it had been his pride to note the increase in these exports. The development of the resources of his colony had been a work in which he had felt that the Colonial Secretary took an immediate interest. He had believed that he was one of the important wheels of the machinery which moved the British Empire: and now, in a day, he was undeceived. It was forced upon him that to the eyes of the outside world he was only a greengrocer operating on a large scale; he provided the British public with coffee for its breakfast, with drugs for its stomach, and with strange woods for its dining-room furniture and walking-sticks. He combated this ignominious character-ization of his position indignantly. The new arrivals certainly gave him no hint that they considered him so lightly. This thought greatly comforted him, for he felt that in some way he was summoning to his aid all of his assets and resources to meet an expert and final valuation. As he ranged them before him he was disturbed and happy to find that the value he placed upon them was the value they would have in the eyes of a young girl — not a girl of the shy, mother-obeying, man-worshipping English type, but a girl such as Miss Cameron seemed to be, a girl who could understand what you were trying to say before you said it, who could take an interest in rates of exchange and preside at a dinner table, who was charmingly feminine and clever, and who was respectful of herself and of others. In fact, he decided, with a flush, that Miss Cameron herself was the young girl he had in his mind.

"Why not?" he asked.

The question came to him in his room, the sixth night of their visit, and he strode over to the long pier-glass and stood studying himself critically for the first time in years. He was still a fine-looking, well-kept man. His hair was thin, but that fact did not show; and his waist was lost, but riding and tennis would set that right. He had means outside of his official salary, and there was the title, such as it was. Lady Greville the wife of the birthday knight sounded as well as Lady Greville the marchioness. And Americans cared for these things. He doubted whether this particular American would do so, but he was adding up all he had to offer, and that was one of the assets. He was sure she would not be

content to remain mistress of the Windless
Isles. Nor, indeed, did he longer care to
be master there, now that he had inhaled
this quick, stirring breath from the outer
world. He would resign, and return and
mix with the world again. He would enter
Parliament; a man so well acquainted as
himself with the Gold Coast of Africa and
with the trade of the West Indies must
always be of value in the Lower House.
This value would be recognized, no doubt,
and he would become at first an Under-
Secretary for the Colonies, and then, in
time, Colonial Secretary and a cabinet minister. She would like that, he thought. And
after that place had been reached, all things
were possible. For years he had not dreamed
such dreams — not since he had been a clerk
in the Foreign Office. They seemed just as
possible now as they had seemed real then,
and just as near. He felt it was all absolutely
in his own hands.

He descended to the dining-room with the
air of a man who already felt the cares of
high responsibility upon his shoulders. His
head was erect and his chest thrown forward.

The Vagrant

He was ten years younger; his manner was alert, assured, and gracious. As he passed through the halls he was impatient of the familiar settings of Government House; they seemed to him like the furnishings of a hotel where he had paid his bill, and where his luggage was lying strapped for departure in the hallway.

In his library he saw on his table a number of papers lying open waiting for his signature, the dog-tax among the others. He smiled to remember how important it had seemed to him in the past — in that past of indolence and easy content. Now he was on fire to put this rekindled ambition to work, to tell the woman who had lighted it that it was all from her and for her, that without her he had existed, that now he had begun to live.

They had never found him so delighful as he appeared that night. He was like a man on the eve of a holiday. He made a jest of his past efforts; he made them see, as he now saw it for the first time, that side of the life of the Windless Isles which was narrow and petty, even ridiculous. He talked of big men in a big way; he criti-

181

cised, and expounded, and advanced his own theories of government and the proper control of an empire.

Collier, who had returned from his unsuccessful search of the plantations, shook his head.

" It's a pity you are not in London now," he said, sincerely. " They need some one there who has been on the spot. They can't direct the colonies from what they know of them in Whitehall."

Sir Charles fingered the dinner cloth nervously, and when he spoke, fixed his eyes anxiously upon Miss Cameron.

" Do you know," he said, "I have been thinking of doing that very thing, of resigning my post here and going back, entering Parliament, and all the rest of it."

His declaration met with a unanimous chorus of delight. Miss Cameron nodded her head with eager approval.

"Yes, if I were a man, that is where I should wish to be," she said, " at the heart of it. Why, whatever you say in the House of Commons is heard all over the world the next morning."

The Vagrant

Sir Charles felt the blood tingle in his pulses. He had not been so stirred in years. Her words ran to his head like wine.

Mr. Collier raised his glass.

" Here's to our next meeting," he said, " on the terrace of the House of Commons."

But Miss Cameron interrupted. " No; to the Colonial Secretary," she amended.

" Oh yes," they assented, rising, and so drank his health, smiling down upon him with kind, friendly glances and good-will.

" To the Colonial Secretary," they said. Sir Charles clasped the arms of his chair tightly with his hands; his eyes were half closed, and his lips pressed into a grim, confident smile. He felt that a single word from her would make all that they suggested possible. If she cared for such things, they were hers; he had them to give; they were ready lying at her feet. He knew that the power had always been with him, lying dormant in his heart and brain. It had only waited for the touch of the Princess to wake it into life.

The American visitors were to sail for the mainland the next day, but he had come to

know them so well in the brief period of their
visit that he felt he dared speak to her that
same night. At least he could give her some
word that would keep him in her mind until
they met again in London, or until she had
considered her answer. He could not expect
her to answer at once. She could take much
time. What else had he to do now but to
wait for her answer? It was now all that
made life.

Collier and his wife had left the veranda
and had crossed the lawn towards the water's
edge. The moonlight fell full upon them
with all the splendor of the tropics, and lit
the night with a brilliant, dazzling radiance.
From where Miss Cameron sat on the veranda in the shadow, Sir Charles could see
only the white outline of her figure and the
indolent movement of her fan. Collier had
left his wife and was returning slowly towards
the step. Sir Charles felt that if he meant to
speak he must speak now, and quickly. He
rose and placed himself beside her in the
shadow, and the girl turned her head inquir-
ingly and looked up at him.

But on the instant the hush of the night

was broken by a sharp challenge, and the sound of men's voices raised in anger; there was the noise of a struggle on the gravel, and from the corner of the house the two sentries came running, dragging between them a slight figure that fought and wrestled to be free.

Sir Charles exclaimed with indignant impatience, and turning, strode quickly to the head of the steps.

"What does this mean?" he demanded. "What are you doing with that man? Why did you bring him here?"

As the soldiers straightened to attention, their prisoner ceased to struggle, and stood with his head bent on his chest. His sombrero was pulled down low across his forehead.

"He was crawling through the bushes, Sir Charles," the soldier panted, "watching that gentleman, sir," — he nodded over his shoulder towards Collier. "I challenged, and he jumped to run, and we collared him. He resisted, Sir Charles."

The mind of the Governor was concerned with other matters than trespassers.

"Well, take him to the barracks, then," he

said. " Report to me in the morning. That
will do."

The prisoner wheeled eagerly, without
further show of resistance, and the soldiers
closed in on him on either side. But as the
three men moved away together, their faces,
which had been in shadow, were now turned
towards Mr. Collier, who was advancing leisurely, and with silent footsteps, across the
grass. He met them face to face, and as he
did so the prisoner sprang back and threw
out his arms in front of him, with the gesture
of a man who entreats silence. Mr. Collier
halted as though struck to stone, and the two
men confronted each other without moving.

" Good God ! " Mr. Collier whispered.

He turned stiffly and slowly, as though in
a trance, and beckoned to his wife, who had
followed him.

" Alice ! " he called. He stepped back-
wards towards her, and taking her hand in
one of his, drew her towards the prisoner.
" Here he is ! " he said.

They heard her cry " Henry ! " with the
fierceness of a call for help, and saw her rush
forward and stumble into the arms of the

prisoner, and their two heads were bent close together.

Collier ran up the steps and explained breathlessly.

"And now," he gasped, in conclusion, "what's to be done? What's he arrested for? Is it bailable? What?"

"Good heavens!" exclaimed Sir Charles, miserably. "It is my fault entirely. I assure you I had no idea. How could I? But I should have known, I should have guessed it." He dismissed the sentries with a gesture. "That will do," he said. "Return to your posts."

Mr. Collier laughed with relief.

"Then it is not serious?" he asked.

"He — he had no money, that was all," exclaimed Sir Charles. "Serious? Certainly not. Upon my word, I'm sorry —"

The young man had released himself from his sister's embrace, and was coming towards them; and Sir Charles, eager to redeem himself, advanced hurriedly to greet him. But the young man did not see him; he was looking past him up the steps to where Miss Cameron stood in the shadow.

Sir Charles hesitated and drew back. The
young man stopped at the foot of the steps,
and stood with his head raised, staring up at
the white figure of the girl, who came slowly
forward.

It was forced upon Sir Charles that in
spite of the fact that the young man before
them had but just then been rescued from
arrest, that in spite of his mean garments and
ragged sandals, something about him — the
glamour that surrounds the prodigal, or possibly the moonlight — gave him an air of
great dignity and distinction.

As Miss Cameron descended the stairs, Sir
Charles recognized for the first time that the
young man was remarkably handsome, and
he resented it. It hurt him, as did also the
prodigal's youth and his assured bearing.
He felt a sudden sinking fear, a weakening
of all his vital forces, and he drew in his
breath slowly and deeply. But no one noticed
him; they were looking at the tall figure of
the prodigal, standing with his hat at his hip
and his head thrown back, holding the girl
with his eyes.

Collier touched Sir Charles on the arm,

The young man stood staring up at the white figure of the girl.

and nodded his head towards the library. "Come," he whispered, "let us old people leave them together. They've a good deal to say." Sir Charles obeyed in silence, and crossing the library to the great oak chair, seated himself and leaned wearily on the table before him. He picked up one of the goose quills and began separating it into little pieces. Mr. Collier was pacing up and down, biting excitedly on the end of his cigar. "Well, this has certainly been a great night," he said. "And it is all due to you, Sir Charles — all due to you. Yes, they have you to thank for it."

"They?" said Sir Charles. He knew that it had to come. He wanted the man to strike quickly.

"They? Yes — Florence Cameron and Henry," Mr. Collier answered. "Henry went away because she wouldn't marry him. She didn't care for him then, but afterwards she cared. Now they're reunited, — and so they're happy; and my wife is more than happy, and I won't have to bother any more; and it's all right, and all through you."

"I am glad," said Sir Charles. There was a long pause, which the men, each deep in his own thoughts, did not notice.

"You will be leaving now, I suppose?" Sir Charles asked. He was looking down, examining the broken pen in his hand.

Mr. Collier stopped in his walk and considered. "Yes, I suppose they will want to get back," he said. "I shall be sorry myself. And you? What will you do?"

Sir Charles started slightly. He had not yet thought what he would do. His eyes wandered over the neglected work, which had accumulated on the desk before him. Only an hour before he had thought of it as petty and little, as something unworthy of his energy. Since that time what change had taken place in him?

For him everything had changed, he answered, but in him there had been no change; and if this thing which the girl had brought into his life had meant the best in life, it must always mean that. She had been an inspiration; she must remain his spring of action. Was he a slave, he asked himself, that he should rebel? Was he a boy, that he could turn his love to aught but the best account? He must remember her not as the woman who had crushed his spirit, but as she who had helped him, who had lifted him up to something better and finer. He would make sacrifice in her name; it would be in her name that he would rise to high places and accomplish much good.

She would not know this, but he would know.

He rose and brushed the papers away from him with an impatient sweep of the hand.

"I shall follow out the plan of which I spoke at dinner," he answered. "I shall resign here, and return home and enter Parliament."

Mr. Collier laughed admiringly. "I love the way you English take your share of public life," he said, "the way you spend yourselves for your country, and give your brains, your lives, everything you have — all for the empire."

Through the open window Sir Charles saw Miss Cameron half hidden by the vines of the veranda. The moonlight falling about her transformed her into a figure which was ideal, mysterious, and elusive, like a woman in a dream. He shook his head wearily. "For the empire?" he asked.

The Last Ride Together

A SKETCH CONTAINING THREE POINTS OF VIEW

What the Poet Laureate wrote.

"THERE are girls in the Gold Reef City
There are mothers and children too!
And they cry 'Hurry up for pity!'
So what can a brave man do?

"I suppose we were wrong, were mad men,
Still I think at the Judgment Day,
When God sifts the good from the bad men,
There'll be something more to say."

*What more the Lord Chief Justice found
to say.*

"In this case we know the immediate consequence of your crime. It has been the loss

13   193

of human life, it has been the disturbance of
public peace, it has been the creation of a
certain sense of distrust of public professions
and of public faith. . . . The sentence of this
Court therefore is that, as to you, Leander
Starr Jameson, you be confined for a period
of fifteen months without hard labor; that
you, Sir John Willoughby, have ten months'
imprisonment; and that you, etc., etc."

London Times, July 29th.

*What the Hon. " Reggie " Blake thought
about it.*

"H. M. HOLLOWAY PRISON,
"July 28th.

"I am going to keep a diary while I am in
prison, that is, if they will let me. I never
kept one before because I had n't the time;
when I was home on leave there was too
much going on to bother about it, and when
I was up country I always came back after a
day's riding so tired that I was too sleepy to
write anything. And now that I have the
time, I won't have anything to write about.
I fancy that more things happened to me to-

194

day than are likely to happen again for the next eight months, so I will make this day take up as much room in the diary as it can. I am writing this on the back of the paper the Warder uses for his official reports, while he is hunting up cells to put us in. We came down on him rather unexpectedly and he is nervous.

" Of course, I had prepared myself for this after a fashion, but now I see that somehow I never really did think I would be in here, and all my friends outside, and everything going on just the same as though I was n't alive somewhere. It's like telling yourself that your horse can't possibly pull off a race, so that you won't mind so much if he does n't, but you always feel just as bad when he comes in a loser. A man can't fool himself into thinking one way when he is hoping the other.

" But I am glad it is over, and settled. It was a great bore not knowing your luck and having the thing hanging over your head every morning when you woke up. Indeed it was quite a relief when the counsel got all through arguing over those proclamations, and the Chief Justice summed up, but I nearly went to sleep when I found he was going all over it again to the jury. I did n't understand about those proclamations myself and I 'll lay a fiver the jury did n't either. The Colonel said he did n't. I could n't keep my mind on what Russell was explaining about, and I got to thinking how much old Justice Hawkins looked like the counsel in 'Alice in Wonderland' when they tried the knave of spades for stealing the tarts. He had just the same sort of a beak and the same sort of a wig, and I wondered why he had his wig powdered and the others did n't. Pollock's wig had a hole in the top; you could see it when he bent over to take notes. He was always taking notes. I don't believe he understood about those proclamations either; he never seemed to listen, anyway.

"The Chief Justice certainly did n't love us very much, that 's sure; and he was n't going to let anybody else love us either. I felt quite the Christian Martyr when Sir Edward was speaking in defence. He made it sound as though we were all a lot of Adelphi heroes and ought to be promoted

and have medals, but when Lord Russell
started in to read the Riot Act at us I began
to believe that hanging was too good for me.
I'm sure I never knew I was disturbing the
peace of nations; it seems like such a large
order for a subaltern.

"But the worst was when they made us
stand up before all those people to be sen-
tenced. I must say I felt shaky about the
knees then, not because I was afraid of what
was coming, but because it was the first time
I had ever been pointed out before people,
and made to feel ashamed. And having
those girls there, too, looking at one. That
wasn't just fair to us. It made me feel
about ten years old, and I remembered how
the Head Master used to call me to his desk
and say, ' Blake Senior, two pages of Horace
and keep in bounds for a week.' And then
I heard our names and the months, and my
name and ' eight months' imprisonment,'
and there was a bustle and murmur and the
tipstaves cried, ' Order in the Court,' and
the Judges stood up and shook out their
big red skirts as though they were shaking
off the contamination of our presence and

rustled away, and I sat down, wondering how long eight months was, and wishing they'd given me as much as they gave Jameson.

"They put us in a room together then, and our counsel said how sorry they were, and shook hands, and went off to dinner and left us. I thought they might have waited with us and been a little late for dinner just that once; but no one waited except a lot of costers outside whom we did not know. It was eight o'clock and still quite light when we came out, and there was a line of four-wheelers and a hansom ready for us. I'd been hoping they would take us out by the Strand entrance, just because I'd like to have seen it again, but they marched us instead through the main quadrangle — a beastly, gloomy courtyard that echoed, and out, into Carey Street — such a dirty, gloomy street. The costers and clerks set up a sort of a cheer when we came out, and one of them cried, 'God bless you, sir,' to the doctor, but I was sorry they cheered. It seemed like kicking against the umpire's decision. The Colonel and I got into a hansom together and we trotted off into Chancery Lane and turned into Holborn. Most of the shops were closed, and the streets looked empty, but there was a lighted clock-face over Mooney's public-house, and the hands stood at a quarter past eight. I didn't know where Holloway was, and was hoping they would have to take us through some decent streets to reach it; but we didn't see a part of the city that meant anything to me, or that I would choose to travel through again.

"Neither of us talked, and I imagined that the people in the streets knew we were going to prison, and I kept my eyes on the enamel card on the back of the apron. I suppose I read, ' Two-wheeled hackney carriage : if hired and discharged within the four-mile limit, 1s.' at least a hundred times. I got more sensible after a bit, and when we had turned into Gray's Inn Road I looked up and saw a tram in front of us with ' Holloway Road and King's X,' painted on the steps, and the Colonel saw it about the same time I fancy, for we each looked at the other, and the Colonel raised his eyebrows.

It showed us that at least the cabman knew where we were going.

"'They might have taken us for a turn through the West End first, I think,' the Colonel said. 'I'd like to have had a look around, would n't you? This is n't a cheerful neighborhood, is it?'

"There were a lot of children playing in St. Andrew's Gardens, and a crowd of them ran out just as we passed, shrieking and laughing over nothing, the way kiddies do, and that was about the only pleasant sight in the ride. I had quite a turn when we came to the New Hospital just beyond, for I thought it was Holloway, and it came over me what eight months in such a place meant. I believe if I had n't pulled myself up sharp, I'd have jumped out into the street and run away. It did n't last more than a few seconds, but I don't want any more like them. I was afraid, afraid — there's no use pretending it was anything else. I was in a dumb, silly funk, and I turned sick inside and shook, as I have seen a horse shake when he shies at nothing and sweats and trembles down his sides.

The Last Ride Together

"During those few seconds it seemed to be more than I could stand; I felt sure that I could n't do it — that I 'd go mad if they tried to force me. The idea was so terrible — of not being master over your own legs and arms, to have your flesh and blood and what brains God gave you buried alive in stone walls as though they were in a safe with a time-lock on the door set for eight months ahead. There 's nothing to be afraid of in a stone wall really, but it 's the idea of the thing — of not being free to move about, especially to a chap that has always lived in the open as I have, and has had men under him. It was no wonder I was in a funk for a minute. I 'll bet a fiver the others were, too, if they 'll only own up to it. I don't mean for long, but just when the idea first laid hold of them. Anyway, it was a good lesson to me, and if I catch myself thinking of it again I 'll whistle, or talk to myself out loud and think of something cheerful. And I don't mean to be one of those chaps who spends his time in jail counting the stones in his cell, or training spiders, or measuring how many of his steps make a mile, for madness lies that way. I mean to sit tight and think of all the good times I've had, and go over them in my mind very slowly, so as to make them last longer and remember who was there and what we said, and the jokes and all that; I'll go over house-parties I have been on, and the times I've had in the Riviera, and scouting parties Dr. Jim led up country when we were taking Matabele Land.

"They say that if you're good here they give you things to read after a month or two, and then I can read up all those instructive books that a fellow never does read until he's laid up in bed.

"But that's crowding ahead a bit; I must keep to what happened to-day. We struck York Road at the back of the Great Western Terminus, and I half hoped we might see some chap we knew coming or going away: I would like to have waved my hand to him. It would have been fun to have seen his surprise the next morning when he read in the paper that he had been bowing to jail-birds, and then I would like to have cheated the tipstaves out of just one more friendly good-

The Last Ride Together

by. I wanted to say good-by to somebody,
but I really couldn't feel sorry to see the
last of any one of those we passed in the
streets — they were such a dirty, unhappy-
looking lot, and the railroad wall ran on
forever apparently, and we might have been
in a foreign country for all we knew of it.
There were just sooty gray brick tenements
and gas-works on one side, and the railroad
cutting on the other, and semaphores and
telegraph wires overhead, and smoke and
grime everywhere, it looked exactly like the
sort of street that should lead to a prison,
and it seemed a pity to take a smart hansom
and a good cob into it.

"It was just a bit different from our last
ride together — when we rode through the
night from Krugers-Dorp with hundreds of
horses' hoofs pounding on the soft veldt
behind us, and the carbines clanking against
the stirrups as they swung on the sling belts.
We were being hunted then, harassed on
either side, scurrying for our lives like the
Derby Dog in a race-track when every one
hoots him and no man steps out to help —
we were sick for sleep, sick for food, lashed

The Last Ride Together

by the rain, and we knew that we were beaten; but we were free still, and under open skies with the derricks of the Rand rising like gallows on our left, and Johannesburg only fifteen miles away."

A List of Books By Richard Harding Davis

CHARLES SCRIBNER'S SONS
PUBLISHERS

THE LION AND THE UNICORN. With six illustrations by H. C. CHRISTY. 12mo. $1.25.

It is more than three years since Mr. Davis has published a book of short stories, and this volume contains the work he has done during this time. They are stories of War and Peace, including, in addition to the title one, "On a Fever Ship," "The Man With One Talent," "The Vagrant," and "The Last Ride Together." In this book Mr. Davis returns to the scenes of his early successes.

NOVELS AND STORIES. New edition, in six volumes, each with photogravure frontispiece. *Sold only in sets.* Limp olive leather, gilt tops, small 16mo. $6.00, *net*.

In response to the popular demand this uniform edition, in small tasteful form, of novels and stories by Mr. Davis, has been prepared. No pains have been spared to give the set the stamp of the highest artistic manufacture. The volumes included are: "Gallegher," "Soldiers of Fortune" (two volumes), "Cinderella," "The King's Jackal," and Mr. Davis's new book, "The Lion and the Unicorn."

THE CUBAN AND PORTO RICAN CAMPAIGNS. With many illustrations from photographs and drawings. *Twentieth Thousand.* Crown 8vo. $1.50.

This is much the most vivid and readable of all the books on the war that have appeared so far, and it is full of life and color and incidents that show the sort of stuff of which our soldiers were made. Not even the multitudes of interesting pictures in the book can distract attention from the text, which is saying a good deal. To the very last line, the book is written with a keenness, a vivacity, a skill and a power to thrill and to leave an impression which mark a decided advance over anything that even Mr. Davis has written heretofore. — *Boston Herald.*

THE KING'S JACKAL. With illustrations and a cover design by C. D. GIBSON. *Twenty-fifth Thousand.* 12mo. $1.25.

Mr. Davis has vigorous ideals — he is in love with strength and cleanness, with " grit "and resource, with heroism and courage in men ; with beauty and frankness, with freshness and youth in women ; and, liking these qualities, he also likes writing about them. Hence, to those who are of Mr. Davis's mind (as I am for one), Mr. Davis's books are always welcome. — *The Academy.*

2

SOLDIERS OF FORTUNE. With illustrations and a cover design by C. D. GIBSON. Uniform with "The King's Jackal." *One Hundred and Thirteenth Thousand.* 12mo. $1.50.

Mr. Davis has produced a rousing tale of adventure, with several fine fellows in it, and one woman whom we are glad to know, and who has gone straight to our hearts and made there for herself a corner that we will keep warm, and to which we will turn with pleasure time and again to love her for all her fine traits — most of all, perhaps, for her genius for *camaraderie,* which found so graceful a climax in the kiss she imprinted on the forehead of the young Englishman who had been murdered by his own treacherous troopers. . . . It is not necessary to commend this story, it has won its way already. But to those who have not read it, we can say, " Do so at once." — *The Critic.*

GALLEGHER, AND OTHER STORIES. With cover design by A. B. FROST. Uniform with "The King's Jackal," and "Soldiers of Fortune." *Forty-fourth Thousand.* 12mo, paper, 50 cents; cloth, $1.00.

Mr. Davis's stories are also of the people and for the people ; and their swift, concentrated style makes them grateful reading. Mr. Davis's Fifth Avenue sketches are as unaffected as those of Cherry Street. — *New York Evening Post.*

CINDERELLA, AND OTHER STORIES. With cover design by A. B. WENZELL. Uniform with "The King's Jackal." 12mo. $1.00.

Mr. Davis's aptitude for work of this kind is too well known to need commendation. There is a freshness and brightness about this volume which is very attractive, for he is one of the writers peculiar to the period, to whom dulness would seem to be impossible. There are five sketches in the book, and each is so good in its way that it is not easy to say which is the best. — *Public Opinion.*

STORIES FOR BOYS. Illustrated. 12mo. $1.00.

All the stories have a verve and fire and movement which is just what boys like. — *Boston Transcript.*

It is a fact not generally known, but nevertheless a fact, that Richard Harding Davis began his career as a weaver of stories for boys, his first work appearing in *St. Nicholas.* . . These capital sketches have genuine interest of plot, a hearty, breezy spirit of youth and adventuresomeness which will captivate the special audience that they are addressed to, and will also interest older people. — *Hartford Courant.*

Charles Scribner's Sons

153–157 Fifth Avenue, New York.

4